LISA HELEN GRAY

EVAN

A CARTER BROTHERS SERIES NOVELLA

CONTENTS

Chapter 1   1
Chapter 2   7
Chapter 3   15
Chapter 4   21
Chapter 5   29
Chapter 6   43
Chapter 7   51
Chapter 8   59
Chapter 9   67
Chapter 10   77
Chapter 11   85
Chapter 12   93
Chapter 13   103
Chapter 14   113
Chapter 15   123
Chapter 16   129
Chapter 17   139
Chapter 18   147
Sneek Peek   157

Acknowledgments   161
Also by Lisa Helen Gray   163
About the Author   165

CHAPTER ONE

EVAN

Finding out your mum isn't really your mum after twenty-eight years, isn't the end of the world. What sucks is finding out she's the person who killed your biological mum.

I always knew I was adopted. Or it's what I told myself to excuse being raised by a cold and loveless woman. My grandparents were loving and kind, and nothing like the mother I grew up with. When they sent me away, I didn't know what I had done wrong. I wondered about it for the longest time.

If it wasn't for my sister, Denny, I would have left our home years before I did. Someone had to be there to protect her.

But I failed.

In so many ways.

Not only did I fail to protect her from Vivian—her mum—but I wasn't there to protect her from the evil lurking in our town. I had to step up, stop making the wrong choices, and start making the right ones.

It's what brought me to now. Things in my life needed to change, and I started with my job.

"Are you sure we can't change your mind to stay?" William, my former boss, asks.

He's annoyed he has to find and train someone new to join his team. There aren't many men my age who have my level of training. Or not many who pass my level of training.

After nine years of being that guy for him, it's time for me to leave. I've done it for so long, I've forgotten there's another world out there for me. A world I've yet to really live in.

Nearly losing my sister recently opened my eyes to that. She's getting married soon and has a baby girl. She has a whole life that I'm not a part of, and I want to be.

I also need my own life. That doesn't mean I'm ready for kids or marriage; just that I want more than I do now. I want to settle down and grow roots.

"No, Sir. I need to do this," I tell him for the tenth time this afternoon.

I'd just finished packing my stuff up from my office when I got called into his. He's been at me to stay on since I handed in my notice a month ago. No matter what he's offered, I've declined, though I did promise to finish off my caseload before leaving. It wasn't required of me, but I didn't want to leave with cases still open. I needed something to feel completed.

"Well, I'm sad to see you go," he declares on a breath. "But son, if you ever, and I mean ever, want to come back to the job, there will always be one here waiting for you."

"Thank you, Sir, but I'm invested in the new business."

"Ah, the security bodyguard gig."

I laugh at the bitterness in his tone. He doesn't get why I want to leave to work for the rich and famous. I like protecting people. I was born to do it. Which is why I want to pave my own way with my new business. It's not only about security for the rich and famous, but making sure people have the best security systems. It's something I'm good at; what I'm passionate about. I've always wanted to get in this side of security work.

It doesn't mean I still won't have to do the occasional job where I'll most likely have to spy on someone's cheating spouse or do background checks. One day, I'll get the business to a place where it needs to be, so I won't need to do those things. Until then, I'm happy to do all the shitty jobs.

As it is, we're doing better than most companies like us do in the first few months of starting. We've got some pretty high-paying clients, some security instalments lined up, and a few jobs here and there.

"Look, I need to get going, but I'll see you tonight, right?" I ask as I heft up the last box of my belongings.

"Tonight?" he asks, looking anywhere but at me.

I snort at his attempt to act clueless. He might be good at his job, but there's a reason he doesn't spend time undercover. He can't keep a secret for shit.

"Yeah, tonight. Whoever planned to be the one to take me out for a drink later, doesn't need to bother. I'll just meet you at the Cavan at ten," I admit.

"It was meant to be a surprise," he mutters dryly.

"Then you should have done a better job at hiding it," I retort.

"Fuck! At least act surprised when you get there," he snaps, rubbing a hand down his face.

I laugh and begin to make my way out. "See you later."

Everyone glances up from their desks when I reach the main room. A few lift their chin in acknowledgement whilst others bid me a farewell. I share my appreciation with a subtle nod and keep going until I hit the front, where I walk into a large reception room.

And this is the part of my job I'll never miss. Every day I've clocked in, I've had to see her face and listen to her remarks.

Sally reminds me of a human Barbie. She might seem pretty to some, but there's not much going on between her ears. And it's all fake. Nothing about her is real or genuine. And she's made working here uncomfortable. She's broken marriages, ruined lives, and planted seeds of doubt which good men have lost their jobs over. And all because they never gave her the time of day. She puts on a good act, and she's gotten away with it time and time again.

"Evan," she coos, smirking when she spots me. "We're going to miss you around here. How about we get together tonight and give you a proper send off? We don't have anything standing between us anymore."

I cringe at the thought. I never outright told her to fuck off since I saw what happened to the men who did. I didn't want my reputation to be tarnished or to have sexual harassment accusations recorded in my work file.

"Yeah, I also don't have to worry about losing my job now either, so I can say what I like to you. Fuck off and pester someone else to get your rocks off. There is no man left in there who will fall for your crap, so do everyone a favour and leave."

I leave her standing at her desk with her mouth hanging wide open. I walk out feeling good about it. I've wanted to say it since the very first day she left her underwear in my desk drawer.

Back at my place, it seems my day isn't getting much better. Lexi, a neighbour and a friend, is walking down the path with her date in tow.

Before my sister got kidnapped, I thought Lexi and I were growing closer. I thought, for a minute, we could be more than friends. But when I went in for a kiss, she couldn't back off any quicker. She told me she was dating someone new and asked if we could still be friends.

Friends.

She fed me the line of 'she sees me as her brother' and that was that. As soon as she friend-zoned me, it made me think on it. I realised I saw what I wanted to see because I've been so desperate to settle down. I built it up in my head to be more because she was easy to be around.

That doesn't mean I have to like her new guy. I can still be her friend, even if things are weird between us now.

Needing to get this awkward exchange over with, I jump out of the car and grab my box from the backseat. Lexi's just stepping onto the pavement when I kick the backdoor closed.

"Hey," she greets quietly.

My eyes narrow on their joined hands when I see his clench around hers. The only thing stopping me from calling him out is because I know Lexi needs this. She lost her confidence after her ex-husband beat her pretty badly. Ever since, she's been working to find herself again.

And I know if this prick was hurting her, she'd tell me. She wouldn't fall into the same trap. It took a lot for her to get out when she did with the last one.

We lived next door to each other before. I had been working another case, and although I should have minded my business and kept my head down, I couldn't help but interfere when I heard the domestic. Thankfully, the day I got involved was when my case finally came to an end. It was the worst job I've ever had to take.

Helping Lexi get to safety took my mind off it. All the rage I let build up inside me during the case, I lashed out onto her husband. I won't lie and say I didn't enjoy every single minute of it.

"Hey," I greet, staring boldly at the jerk next to her.

"You remember Simon, don't you?" she asks, sucking in her lower lip.

"Nice to see you again, Steve. I was in a rush the last time," I lie.

I wasn't in a rush. I just didn't like him.

"It's Simon," he growls.

I don't answer. Instead, I glance at Lexi. "I've got to get moving. I've got to meet the lads in an hour," I tell her.

I haven't got to meet them until later tonight, but I don't want to stick around and do idle chit chat.

"Okay, I'll let you get going. Hopefully, I'll see you later," she tells me, and it sounds more like a plea than anything. "Oh, and before I forget, a letter was posted for you at my address a few months back by mistake. I forgot all about it until I was clearing my drawer out. I've left it on your kitchen counter."

"Cheers—"

"You have a key to his apartment?" Steve accuses, aghast.

"Yeah. I told you I look after his place sometimes," she explains.

"I'll see you later," I tell her, and leave before they can drag me into an argument. "See you later, Steve."

"It's Simon," he snaps.

Who the fuck cares?

I continue to walk up the path to the front door. It takes seconds to unlock the front door and let myself in. As I kick it closed, I get a glimpse of them still talking at the end of the path. I should have explained why she has a key to my place. I should have given her an out. But fuck if I give a man like that my attention.

The letter is the first thing I see when I walk into the kitchen, but instead of opening it, I lower the box to the counter and grab a beer from the fridge. The hiss of the can opening is heaven as I make my way into the living room. I've been dying to open one all week, but I had to keep a level head if I wanted to get all my work finished.

I turn the television on and relax back onto the sofa to watch the sports highlights.

For the first time in a long time, I can finally relax. I'm no longer on someone else's clock. I make my own hours. Determine my own rules.

I'm finally free from all the fucked up shit my job entailed.

CHAPTER
TWO

KENNEDY

W hy am I so fudging nervous? He's a policeman. One who specialises in gang crimes, so they aren't loitering about our streets. He took an oath to serve and protect, not blame and shame.

Maybe he'll be overjoyed. He should be.

Or maybe he won't be.

Maybe he will get angry.

I groan at the war going on inside my mind. I'm sitting outside a stranger's house in my beat-up red Rover. I should be grateful my car even made it here.

That has to be a good sign, right?

My car needs so much work done to it, but since it will cost more than the car is worth, it's not worth it. I knew there was a chance I might break down, but it was a risk I was willing to take.

It's now or never.

Banging my head on the steering wheel, I try to calm my nerves.

I can do this.

I tell myself I'm doing the right thing, but a voice in the back of my mind is screaming at me to turn back. I've gone weeks with no replies to my letters or calls. I don't know what I'm hoping to achieve, but I do know we deserve answers as to why. Imogen deserves at least that much.

The pent-up anger I've been bottling up since the first letter was ignored, begins to release. Getting out of the car, I grimace when the rusty door protests loudly. Loud enough to wake the dead.

I tap the hood of the car. "I swear, if you get me back home after this, I'll treat you to some WD40 or something. Maybe even an oil change."

It takes me a few tries to get the door to fully close, and once I do, I'm sweating and out of breath. It's then I realise I've not rolled the window back up, and I want to cry.

Please, just let one thing go right for me.

I pry the door back open and get to work on rolling the window back up. It's not an easy feat since the window came off the runner weeks ago. But with a bit of manoeuvring and practice, I finally get the window rolled up.

Closing the door once again takes me a few tries. I'm surprised no one has come out yet to investigate the sound.

Walking up to the front door is easy. Knocking? That's another flipping story. Biting my bottom lip until I taste blood, I finally find the courage to knock. The sound echoes in my ears.

Anyone would think I was walking to my own death.

When no one answers, I knock again. I know he's here. I waited a few cars down for him to come home. I didn't know what he looked like, but I knew where he lived.

There was a guy who arrived earlier, who I thought might have been Evan. He started walking up the path, towards the house that belonged to the man I had been waiting for. I rolled down the window and listened to him talk crudely to someone over the phone. He was talking about a woman he was going to bang tonight, and his words almost made me want to forget about speaking to him.

But then he detoured to the neighbour's house and I began to relax. It was short-lived when another car pulled up. I knew as soon as he stepped out that it was *him.*

The door is pulled open, and my mouth hangs open. He doesn't look anything like I pictured him to look. He's seriously good looking. He's wearing a white shirt that is untucked, the top few buttons undone, and the tie around his neck is loose. He has his sleeves rolled up, showing the veins on the inside of his arms. I've never understood my arousal to those veins, but something about them just turns me on.

How my sister snagged him is anyone's guess. I don't want to speak ill of the dead, but she wasn't the best person. Dying so young was the best thing to happen to her, and I say that kindly.

Vicky was off the rails for a long time. She liked to blame it on our parents' deaths, but she struggled long before that. I barely remember a time when she wasn't popping pills or smoking weed. She got mixed up in things she shouldn't have and spiralled out of control. No matter what I did, she wouldn't change. I tried everything, but I couldn't save someone who didn't want to be saved.

"Yeah?" he demands, his voice deep and husky. My jaw continues to hang open. "Can I help you?"

Shaking myself out of it, I blurt out, "She's yours!"

I close my eyes at how harsh my words are. I had a big speech prepared, but now I'm standing in front of him, I forget it all.

What the fudge is wrong with me?

"Excuse me?" he asks, arching a brow.

He probably thinks I'm a mental patient. And I wouldn't blame him.

"I... um... I'm Kennedy Wright," I greet, forgetting my anger towards the god-like angel.

A small smirk plays at the corner of his lips, and my gaze is immediately drawn to them. They're full, red, and totally kissable. "I'm Evan, and as entertaining as this is, I still don't know who you are or why you are here."

Butterflies flutter in my stomach, and my body begins to heat.

His tongue reaches out, flicking his top lip, and I sigh.

He coughs, breaking the spell his lips have me under, and I blush furiously. I shake my head, ignoring how incredibly sexy he looks when he grins, and how his muscles look flexing in his white shirt.

"Get it together," I whisper.

"I'm sorry, I didn't catch that."

"Sorry. Look, can I come in?"

"Not to sound rude, Kennedy, but I still don't know why you're here or why you'd be knocking on my door. I'd remember seeing a pretty face like yours before, so I know we haven't hooked up."

He thinks I'm beautiful? I sigh, melting at his words.

I give him a slow smile but soon lose it when I remember why I'm here.

"Do you remember Vicky Wright?" I ask.

"Vicky Wright? Vicky... Vick... Vicky. Fuck!" His eyes narrow on me, so I'm assuming he's just remembered who she is. "Whatever the fuck that fucking bitch wants, I don't want to know about it."

He goes to slam the door, but I move, pushing it back and wedging my foot in the doorway.

"Hold on just a darn minute," I snap, and he stops trying to close it. "I'm not having you do this. You've ignored me for weeks. You had a chance to do this over the phone or by post and not face to face, so you'll hear me out."

"You're as crazy as her," he barks. "Are you... Wait... Wright. You said you were Kennedy Wright. Please tell me she's not your sister, that she didn't make you come here to do her dirty work?"

"Well, since she's dead, I'd say that's a resounding no," I retort.

"Fuck! I'm—"

I hold my hand up, feeling my temper rise. "Please don't say you're sorry when we both know you're not," I argue.

"If she's dead then I don't see why you're here. If she was murdered, or you want someone to look into her death, you'll have to file a report," he explains.

He really doesn't have a clue.

I had an inkling that she was lying, which is why I kept sending the letters. She told me he knew and wanted nothing to do with Imogen. But no one can fake this type of reaction. He truly doesn't know.

"You don't understand. I... um... Do we have to do this outside?" I ask, twiddling my thumbs. My anger simmers, if only for a moment. The only reason I haven't left is because of Imogen. She doesn't deserve this.

"Come in, but if you don't hurry up and tell me what the fuck is going on, I'm going to kick you back out."

I step inside and he closes the front door behind me. The place is small and cosy. An armchair, a sofa, and a TV are in the living room, and to the right is an open plan kitchen. I expected it to be messy in here, but it's tidy.

Maybe he has a girlfriend.

"What is this about?" he asks impatiently.

"It's about Imogen," I begin.

"Who is Imogen?"

"She's a five-month-old baby," I tell him.

"That's... um, great," he mutters dryly. He's still looking at me like I've grown two heads. For a detective, or whatever he is, he sure doesn't know how to connect the dots.

"She's Vicky's. Do the math."

He watches me for a few seconds, not even blinking. I know the minute he clicks on to what I'm saying. His greyish blue eyes turn stormy, and a shiver runs down my spine.

I don't like the look or the vibe he's giving off, so I take a step back, hitting the front door.

"That fucking... If you're insinuating what I think you are then you'll need a DNA test because that bitch spread her legs for pennies."

"You should know," I snap, hating the reminder of what she was like. Most people didn't see just how bad she was, but I did.

"I should know? I should know," he roars, pulling at his fair hair.

I don't know what I expected, but I didn't expect this type of reaction. He's angry, and I'm not sure what he's angry about.

Did he love her that much and is now struggling to believe she would do this to him? Or did he know what she was like, and he's annoyed that she's still messing him around, even after death?

Personally, I never understood why someone with such a good

reputation and job would be interested in an underweight drug user. She was my sister, and I loved her, but she wasn't a good person. She was vile and mean, and had no self-respect at all.

"Look, I'm sorry she isn't the one telling you this. I get you might have feelings for her, but—"

He scoffs. "That slut fucking drugged me. Okay, I don't know if it was her who actually slipped the drugs into my drink, but she definitely was the whore who rode my dick while I was unconscious," he declares in disgust.

My eyes bug out. *Oh my gosh.*

Out of all the things my sister has done, I never expected this to be one of them. She raped him. What she did was rape, and I can't comprehend why she would do such a thing. This is another thing I'll never be able to tell Imogen when she's older. And what do I do if he wants nothing to do with her? What reason can I give her when she's older and she asks me who her dad is?

God, I feel sick.

"I'm sorry she did that to you," I tell him softly, my voice just above a whisper.

He scoffs, looking down at me. "I'm not a victim. She was as messed up as I was, if not worse. But then she was used to it, whereas I had never done a drug in my life." He sits down on the edge of the thick-cushioned sofa, dragging his hand down his face. "How do you know she's mine?"

"She never told me about you. I figured it out for myself when I went through her belongings. All I knew about you was that you were some big shot, and that you were a rat," I admit. I knew what she meant. He's the reason her drug dealer got arrested. I read about it in the paper. "She said you knew. I didn't believe her for a second, but what right did I have to question her? When she died, they handed me her belongings. I read messages between her and a friend, and she told her 'Evan' is her baby's dad. I did some digging after I found out you were undercover and here I am."

He meets my gaze. "I need time to process this. Where is the kid? How old did you say she was?"

"Imogen is five months old. She's been through a lot. She was born an addict, even though Vicky did try to stay off the drugs. It just wasn't enough. In the end, it's what killed her. She signed her parental rights over to me not long after Imogen was born. She died two days later."

I still feel sick thinking about it. She abandoned a sick baby, *her baby*, to go and get her next fix. I'll never get it. She didn't even look back or hesitate. If anything, she looked relieved to be out of there.

"Is the baby okay?" he asks, but he sounds weird, robotic even.

"She is now. She got released six weeks after she was born and now has a clean bill of health. They weaned her off the drugs as soon as she was born. The doctors weren't confident she'd survive because she was also six weeks premature, but she did. They have warned me about development issues but so far none have arisen. She checks out okay."

"Good. Good," he murmurs, and gets up to start pacing. "When can we get the DNA test done?"

I thought for sure he'd never ask for one and I would have to convince him. I didn't expect him to want anything to do with her.

"I actually ordered one for you. I've already got Imogen's ready, but you'll need to do yours. All you have to do is take a swab sample from the inside of your cheek and send it off."

I rummage through my bag until I find the white pre-addressed envelope at the bottom and hand it to him.

"Look, I have to go. I know this has come out of the blue and you'll need some time to digest everything. I just needed to meet you to get answers. As Imogen's legal guardian, I wanted to be able to look her in the eye one day and tell her I tried," I admit, my eyes watering. I grab the other envelope from out of the bag and hand it to him. "There are a few pictures of Imogen in there, and my phone number and address for you to get in contact. Please send that off ASAP and make sure you do it right. If you do it but don't want any part in Imogen's life, I will understand. What Vicky did, who she was, it's not right or fair. But Imogen is innocent in all of this. She didn't ask to be born into it, so for her, please be mindful."

"I'll get them done," he promises, and I get a glimpse of tears in his eyes. "I just... I need some time. I'll do anything you want me to, but I just need some time to process this. If she's mine..."

"It's okay. We can talk more when we get the results back, okay?"

"Okay."

I nod and turn, opening the door. He doesn't see me out, and I don't expect him to. He's just been given some big news. He drops down on the sofa with the envelope in hand and doesn't wait to open it.

I close the door behind me, giving him privacy. The minute it closes, I hear him weeping, and I know he's looking at the image of Imogen hooked up to a bunch of machines in an incubator.

That reaction isn't from a man who wants nothing to do with his daughter. It sounds like a man who needs to process the news because he plans to be her dad.

It's the outcome I've wanted for her from the beginning.

CHAPTER
THREE

EVAN

Aaron sits back down on the stool in front of me, handing me another pint. I've lost count of how many drinks I've had since I arrived an hour ago. All I keep doing is replaying Kennedy's words in my mind.

I'm a dad to a five-month-old baby.

I stared at the pictures she gave me for hours before I realised she'd gone and the sun had gone down. I called Aaron straight away and told him I needed him to meet me.

When we met up, I explained everything, leaving nothing out. We drank. We talked. We drank some more.

And now I'm ready to head over to Kennedy's and demand answers. That said, I know if I go in this state, I will scare her away. She's not like her sister—or at least, that's the vibe I got from her.

I have so many questions, like why she didn't come sooner. What did her sister tell her about me? Fuck! My head is spinning just thinking about it all.

"Fuck, mate. I don't know what to say."

"A baby. A fucking baby. I don't even know if she wants me to take her. She said she came for answers, but what if that wasn't about answers at all? I don't know how to look after a baby. What if she is mine and I'm wasting more weeks until the results come in not being with her?" I ramble, scrubbing my hands down my face. I'm still in my work clothes.

Since Kennedy's visit, everything just seems to be going downhill. My mind is torn about what to do. Do I stay away until the results are in or do I go see her? It's more time I'll miss if I wait around, but then I don't want to get attached, only to have her ripped away from me in a second.

For fuck's sake.

I thought the woman was there to hit on me, or that she was some sort of stripper the guys had hired. I wouldn't put it past my ex work colleagues to do something like that. She looked so fucking cute, all flustered and shy, yet staring at me like she was trying to find the first place to lick. Her flustered reaction gave away the fact she wasn't a stripper. Looks wise, she was a fucking knockout, and could easily work a pole.

Then she got feisty, pushing me with her dainty finger, like a little pixie, all small and shit. Her fucking eyes were the colour of melted chocolate. They were deep, rich, and so fucking sexy I wanted to drag her back to my room and do unspeakable things to her.

"Man, you'll figure this shit out. It probably ain't your kid anyway," he tells me.

I swear he's had that exact speech on repeat since I told him the news. Aaron is my best mate. I'd jump in front of a bullet for him. In fact, he'd do the same for me. But when it comes to advice, he really does fucking suck.

I'd have gone to my sister but we still aren't in a great place. I kept so much from her, and I wasn't there for her when she needed me the most. Now I need her, and it seems selfish to expect her to be there for me.

I wouldn't blame her if she never spoke to me again. I could have prevented Carl from taking her. I knew he was up to something, but I chose to see what he would do first. And because of that, he managed to evade our observations and kidnap her. If I knew my sister was in his clutches, I would have been there. But I didn't get the full story until the damage was already done.

I've sent her bloke, Mason, a message tonight, asking him to talk to her on my behalf. I need her, and I hate this space she's put between us. One day, she'll understand why I did what I did, but until then, I have to deal with the consequences of my actions.

He agreed to speak to her, but told me not to push it and to let her process everything.

I hate to admit this, but he's good for her. I didn't like it at first because the lad has slept with more people than the entire police department put together. He's a fucking animal. Or he was.

I've been keeping an eye on him when he's not with Denny, just in case. I don't want her to be hurt again. So far, the lad doesn't even blink in another girl's direction.

It's a fucking miracle after the rumours I've heard about him.

My sister, though, she's a game changer. She's kind, sweet, loving, and is one of those people who doesn't want you to change to fit her mould. She wants people to be themselves.

"I don't fucking know," I groan, my thoughts directing back to Kennedy and the little girl.

My little girl.

There was something in the way Kennedy looked at me, or the way she spoke about Imogen, but I truly do believe this kid is mine.

I wouldn't have felt as strongly as I did when she announced it otherwise. The news rocked through my body, and I just knew. I don't fucking know how, but I did.

I scrub a hand over my face, hoping I'm not being fooled by a pretty face. She could be just like her sister, even if my head is telling me she isn't.

The tests will be done soon, and I'll have answers. A part of me wants her to be mine because I don't want to imagine who her father is otherwise. Most of the blokes who went through that unit were the worst of the worst. That little girl deserves more than a scumbag for a father, since her mother was a whore who caused her to be born an addict.

"Well, drink up. Everyone just walked in," Aaron announces, and I straighten on my stool.

"It's supposed to be a fucking surprise. We said eight, dipshit," William belts out, glaring at Aaron.

My laugh is forced, but it's all I can muster right now. "Oh, I'm surprised," I reply. Just not about this.

He slaps me on my back, and I decide to push my thoughts aside, concentrating on the night instead. They went to the trouble to organise this send off, so I'll pull up my trousers and drink until I forget everything else going on in my life.

Aaron holds his hands up in defence. "He called me to meet him here. Who am I to refuse?"

"Useless fucking shit," William mutters, then steps out of the way when Dave walks over with a tray of Jagerbombs.

"Shots!" Dave yells, and I grimace, taking one from the tray.

I wince when the music gets turned up a notch.

God, I'm getting old.

Just when I think the night is getting better, the fucking reception slut walks in with one of the new lads. I think his name is Mikey, but I'm unsure since I never got the chance to speak to him. He's hanging on to her every word as they approach.

Poor fucker is going to regret it once he gets to know her better— or worse, sleeps with her.

Aaron notices where I'm looking and groans.

"I swear, I didn't invite the bitch," he assures me. "But if it helps, I'll put twenty on it not lasting another hour. The poor fuck looks miserable."

I look again and notice he does look fucking miserable. He's eyeing up one of the women who have been standing up by the bar all night.

"Half an hour, and make it thirty," I banter, shaking his hand.

Another tray of shots appears and I know I'm in for a long night.

Kidneys, may you rest in peace, my friends.

———

The night is coming to an end, and it's one in the morning when the guys finally carry me out of the pub.

"I'm never drinking again," I whine, my words slurring together.

"That's what you said the last time we went out," someone remarks, laughing.

I don't find it funny though. I've never been a big drinker, and tonight, I drank my body weight.

Everything around me is a blur of colour, and I feel like I'm spinning.

"Let's get you home," William rumbles, sounding as sober as me.

I'm shoved into a taxi, and Aaron hops in beside me, giving the driver my address.

I must fall asleep because I'm shaken awake when we pull up outside mine. "You kipping at mine?" I ask Aaron.

"Yeah, mate. Wouldn't want you to choke on your own vomit now, would we?"

"If he's sick in my cab, you pay," the driver shouts.

"I'm kidding," Aaron remarks, snorting.

"He's not. I feel green," I joke, but end up gagging on my words.

"You—you get out my taxi," the driver orders.

"We're going, we're going," Aaron assures him.

The minute the door closes behind us, the taxi speeds off, tyres screeching on the tarmac.

"Ha! Joke's on that fucker. We haven't paid," Aaron hoots.

"Ha! Take that, ya fucker," I muse, glancing down the street. He's no longer in sight, but I don't care.

"Come on, Rocky," Aaron teases.

He drags me up the path at the same time Lexi opens her front door.

"Is everything okay?" she asks timidly, her eyes scanning Aaron up and down. They've met a few times so I'm used to this interaction, but fuck me if I don't roll my eyes.

"Peachy. Why don't you go back to Steve," I tell her snarkily, wondering why her life got so perfect while mine got so fucked up.

"Um, it's Simon, and we broke up," she reveals softly.

I groan, feeling like shit. As much of a jerk Steve was, she doesn't deserve to go through this.

We stumble inside, and I have to grip the door to stop myself from falling over. "Sorry. The guy was a dick. You can do better."

"Yeah, he was," she agrees, her lashes lowering with concern.

"Well, I'm going to bed. You two play nice," I order, before walking head first into the doorframe. I rub at the bruises forming. "Fuck! Who put that there?"

"Careful, mate," Aaron teases.

I glower at him, moving down the hallway to my bedroom, grateful I don't have stairs. I don't think I'm capable of navigating them right now.

I drop down on the bed, shoving my face into the pillow when I hear them both talking. He mentions coffee, to which Lexi agrees, so I grab the other pillow, throwing it to the door so it closes.

Once their yapping is drowned out, and the room stops spinning, I close my eyes, letting sleep pull me under.

My last thought before everything goes dark is of the baby I'm still yet to meet.

CHAPTER
FOUR

KENNEDY

Uncontrollable wailing echoes in my ear as I rock Imogen in my arms.

"Come on, baby girl, go to sleep," I coo softly.

She started teething the past few nights, and no matter how many freaking textbooks or articles online that I've read, nothing seems to be working.

She has barely rested for days, and my heart is literally breaking over hearing her in pain. I've gotten good at deciphering her cries. Each one sounds different and is for different things. Yet tonight, I can't tell what is bothering her more: her teeth coming through, or if there's something else going on.

She cries loudly, pulling at her ears, which turned a dark shade of red over an hour ago.

"Please, Imogen," I plead, lowering myself into the rocking chair so I can take her temperature again.

The thermometer beeps, and I turn the device to see it's just a little over the norm. It still doesn't ease my worry.

Knowing I'm not going to be able to get much sleep this morning, I start rocking backwards and forwards in the chair. The lyrics to Meghan Trainor's *All About That Bass* roll out of my mouth as I try to soothe her. It's the first song to pop into my head, but my girl loves her music.

After the first verse, she starts to settle. Her tiny but chubby fist is shoved into her mouth, the other still holding on to her ear.

Thankfully, it's not long before she's asleep, and I place her gently down in her cot. I'm glad I don't have to work this week. I had some annual leave left, and it felt right using it with Imogen being so poorly. I can't afford to have any unpaid time off.

After tiptoeing out of her tiny room so I don't wake her, I walk back through my small, two-bedroomed flat, to the kitchen. The place isn't ideal, but it's the only place I could find that was affordable.

It's located in one of the roughest places in town, and I do hate it here. I'm never able to get a full night's sleep due to loud music coming from other floors, or because some couple decided tonight's the night to get into a fight. It echoes through the walls day and night, making it unbearable.

Loud banging at the door has me jumping out of my skin. I quickly drop the washing-up liquid and run to the door before they can wake up Imogen.

I'm hoping like hell it's not my creepy neighbour from down the hall. I'm pretty sure his creep factor is because he does drugs and can't separate reality from his tripping.

He's always knocking on my door for sugar. It's never for anything else. At first, I thought it was to see what valuables were lying around that he could steal, but my home has never been broken into. There isn't anything worth stealing anyway. The only things worth stealing is my mum's jewellery, but I keep that safely locked away under my bed. The rest of the stuff is second-hand that I picked up from charity shops or had donated to me.

I pull open the door, too tired to deal with him. "I don't have any spare—"

My words are cut off when a large hand wraps around my throat, pushing me back into the flat. He's squeezing so tight, I don't have a chance to breathe in and scream.

The door slams closed, and my heart stops, hoping it doesn't wake Imogen up. I don't want whoever this is to know she's here.

I shake uncontrollably as I claw at the man's wrists, but my hands go limp when he slams me against my bedroom door, his red-rimmed eyes boring into me.

"Where's my fucking money, bitch?"

I try to talk, but his hand is cutting off my air supply. I frantically claw at his wrists to get him to loosen his hold, but it never happens. Wheezing noises start to leave my mouth, and panic grows within me.

What the hell is happening? Who is he? What money? Does he think I'm someone else?

My mind races with all these questions as I scan the room for something to hit him with. Everything is out of my reach, and his grip is too strong for me to get free.

My vision begins to blur just as he drops me to the floor. I stumble back a few steps, my mind frozen as I gasp for breath. I don't even have a chance to think, or to speak, before his hand clashes with my cheek. Pain radiates down my face, tears falling free as I cry out.

"Please," I beg, for what I'm not sure.

This has to be a misunderstanding.

I'm not the person he's looking for.

"Get the fuck up, bitch," he sneers.

When I don't move fast enough, he grips me by the hair, lifting me and pinning me back to the door. The force of my hip hitting the metal handle has me screaming out.

His fingers dig into my cheeks, touching the same place he hit only moments ago. It throbs, and I can already tell it's beginning to swell. It feels like I have an orange stuck on the inside of my cheek.

I'm paralysed, his menacing aura pinning me in a frightening grip. A cold wave slivers over me as the hairs rise on the nape of my neck. My body shivers from it.

How could someone do this to someone else?

"Please, I don't know who you are," I cry, my words ending on a squeak as he tightens his grip.

"Your sister owes me three grand. I want my fucking money, bitch."

Vicky.

Dread plummets in my stomach as everything begins to make sense.

A few months after my sister died, I started to receive letters demanding money. They weren't addressed to anyone, so I threw them out, assuming whoever delivered them just got the wrong address.

I didn't think much of it because I was too worried about Imogen making it through. She was still in intensive care at that point, and it was touch and go.

"She's... She's dead," I wheeze out, my voice hitching.

"I know that, you fucking whore. You're my payment. You were what your sister put down as, shall we call it, a *guarantor*," he snickers.

"I don't understand," I whisper, feeling bile rise in my throat.

I don't have that kind of money. I live by my monthly wages, and that's it. I don't have any kind of savings anywhere.

"Let me make this clear; this was a friendly visit. The next time I come and you don't have my money, you'll fucking pay in the worst way."

His dead eyes bore into me, and I know he's serious. What did I ever do to deserve this and why would my *sister* do this to me?

Before I can explain the situation, he throws me to the floor with force. I land on the coffee table, the cheap wood breaking under my weight.

Coughing, I roll onto my side, only for his boot to land in my ribs.

"Please stop. Someone, help!" I scream, finding my voice.

He continues to kick, each blow making my insides turn. Just when I think he'll never stop, he does, kneeling down until his face is only inches away from mine.

Unbearable pain spreads through my entire body as I meet his gaze.

"You've got a month to get me that fucking money," he demands, gripping my cheeks in a vice. "If you don't, that little brat in there is going to be fucking sold to the highest bidder."

No!

Even without seeing into the future, I know I won't be enough to save her. People like him—violent criminals—are cruel. They lack empathy and will not struggle to do what he threatened.

But I will die trying to save her.

Before I can fight back, or get to Imogen, he swings his fist back. The last thing I see before he takes his shot is his fist coming right at me.

———

Gentle hands are slowly rubbing my shoulders, stirring me awake. Agonising pain races up my spine and through the rest of my body as I blink my eyelids open.

I startle, ready to scream and lash out as it all comes back to me, but relax when I see it's only Melanie—my neighbour who lives across the hall.

I scan the room, searching for the man who attacked me, but it's only us. Imogen begins to cry, and I crawl to my knees, wheezing through the agony that courses through me.

"Don't move," she stresses.

"Imogen," I breathe, hearing her cry.

Looking torn, she reluctantly gets to her feet. "Don't move. I'll get her, Kennedy."

Grateful she came, I sit up and rest against the sofa, unable to do much more. Melanie has been the only neighbour I've got on with in these flats. She's not only my friend; she's a lifesaver. She is always here for me.

She walks in with Imogen still crying in her arms. When I put my hands up for her, I forget my injuries for a second. I hiss out, and dots cloud my vision as I breathe through the discomfort.

"I've got her," she assures me, rocking her side to side. "What happened, Kennedy? Shall I call the police? Or an ambulance?"

I shake my head. "Please don't," I plead.

I don't know whether going to the police will make it worse or not. I don't have any proof, or even know the guy's name. All I know is that it has something to do with my sister. And since I don't exactly live in a place that has the best security, there's nothing more I can do. I'm pretty sure the cameras are just for show.

From past experiences, I know there isn't much they can do either. Or they couldn't when my sister robbed money from me. Nor when she stole a car at seventeen. I knew it was her, but it was my word against hers.

"What are you doing here?" I ask, trying hard to keep the tears at bay. Melanie said she was leaving for a few weeks for a job. She wasn't meant to be back for another week.

"I'll tell you later," she replies before handing me a white envelope. "This was delivered to mine sometime during the week, which is why I'm here."

Mindful not to move too quickly, I glance at the envelope, my eyes widening. "Oh my god," I breathe, tearing it open.

I scan the page that is filled with numbers and words I don't understand, but I keep going until I reach the centre, where it states in bold letters who Imogen's father is.

The force of what it truly means hits me, and I clench the paper in my hand.

"What is it?" Melanie asks, finally soothing Imogen.

I meet her gaze, knowing this is the best thing that could have happened.

"He's her dad," I reveal, since she knows about the paternity test.

He can protect her.

Knowing it means I will lose her, I lower my head. The thought of never seeing her again scares me, but it's what I might need to do to save her. I won't let that man take her from me.

I hold my hands out, needing to hold her as tears stream down my cheeks. Melanie reluctantly hands her over, and my body screams in agony at the pressure.

I breathe in her baby scent and burst into tears.

"It's okay, baby. Everything is going to be okay. I'll protect you, I promise," I swear, even though I know it means I have to give her up.

"What is going on, Kennedy?" Melanie asks, sitting down next to me. "Who did this to you? I ran to get some ice from mine, but it seems neither of us have anything frozen." Her tone sounds light, but I can hear the underlying worry hidden beneath.

"Someone... Someone attacked me. He wants money. Money I don't have. He's going to take Imogen if I don't pay him," I admit, experiencing the same paralysing fear I got earlier when he threatened me.

She gently places her hand over mine. "Has this got anything to do with your sister?" she asks, knowing all about Vicky.

She was there every time Vicky would show up asking for money. She was here the day Vicky told me she was pregnant. And she was there for me when I got back from the hospital, and helped me transition into motherhood. She has raised two kids of her own, both of which now have families of their own. Still, despite the age difference between us, she has been the friend I needed and vice versa.

"I'm scared," I admit, and gently run my finger down Imogen's cheek when she begins to fuss. "It's okay, Imogen. I will keep you safe. I promise."

And I hope to God that I'm right.

"What the fuck has happened here?" is yelled, and my entire body locks up.

He's come back to finish me off.

I clutch Imogen to my chest, blocking her from the assault, but nothing comes. I glance to the door, and my eyes well up with tears when I see the person I need right now.

"*Evan,*" I breathe.

CHAPTER
FIVE

EVAN

t's been weeks since I sent off the DNA test, and even though I
knew it would take some time, I never thought it would be this
long.

"You need to snap out of it, mate. You've been off with the fairies
for weeks," Harris—another one of my best mates—tells me.

He doesn't even realise how close he is about the fairy comment.
I've not been able to stop myself from thinking about Kennedy or
Imogen, and Kennedy reminds me of a fairy.

"I'm just going to go home. I'm sorry."

"It's okay. You can take the week off anyway. I'll get everything
sorted here, so just make sure you get your head cleared before you
come back." I go to interrupt but he stops me, holding his hand up.
"This is how accidents happen, Evan. Your head isn't in the game."

"I know. Just give me a few days," I declare, before leaving him to
fill out the paperwork on the court's file.

I'm pulling up outside mine and a sense of Deja vu hits me when I
see Lexi walking down the path, hand in hand with some new tool.
What surprises me is that it isn't Aaron. After the night I got

completely wasted, I thought for sure I had imagined hearing her tell me they broke it off.

Guess it really did happen.

I jump out of the car and give her a chin lift, not wanting to go through the same pleasantries as last time.

"Hey," she greets, and I notice the tool looking at me like I'm competition.

Don't worry, loser, I have enough problems.

"Hey," I greet back.

"This is Steve," she introduces, and I want to groan and look to the sky. Why does she constantly put me through this shit?

"I need to run in and get a file, but it's good to see you, and you, Simon," I announce, before brushing past them.

"It's Steve," he corrects, and I shake my head, not giving a fuck.

I let myself in and notice the mail on the floor. I gather the pile, and begin to flick through them.

"Bills, junk, bills, bills, junk, wrong address, junk, junk—oh fuck," I pause when I get to the last one, seeing where it's from.

This is the letter I've been waiting for. I tear it open, but the minute I hold the piece of paper in my hand, I freeze.

Although I want her to be mine, there's a part of me that doesn't want her to be. When I pictured having children, I saw it being with a woman I loved and was settled down with—not someone who took advantage of me.

Closing my eyes, I let go of my troubles, knowing there is nothing I can do to change it. I count to ten whilst I open the letter up, before finally glancing down at the paper.

Not much of it makes sense, not until I see in bold letters that I am Imogen Wright's biological father.

"Fuck!"

I've spent weeks stressing over whether she is mine or not. I've not really given too much thought as to what it means or what is expected of me. Not really.

But now I know, I need to meet her. I grab my keys from the counter, along with the letter and the pictures of Imogen, and head back out. I don't want to waste another minute of her life. I've already missed too much.

She might not have been my child by choice, or with a woman I loved, but she is still my daughter.

And I'm going to be the best fucking dad. Or fail trying.

————

So far, I've only doubted my decision to show up unannounced twice. I have Kennedy's number, but I didn't know what to say. And I didn't want her to change her mind about letting me see my daughter.

Then I regretted leaving without a gift, so I stopped off at a shop and grabbed the fluffiest pink pony teddy bear I could find. I knew she'd never know if I got her something or not, but I would know. And it felt wrong turning up without a gift.

I still can't believe I'm a dad. It still feels foreign to me, and I can't truly process it. But the one thing I do know is, I will never end up like my father. He might be redeeming himself now, but that doesn't make up for the years he neglected us and left us to survive the wrath of Vivian. Nothing could make up for it. I never want Imogen to be in the place we are now, where she has to forgive and forget. Because I know from experience, you can forgive, but there's nothing you can do to forget.

It's only when I pull into an estate that I realise where she lives. It never registered to me before, not even when I put it in my satnav. It's one of the worst places to live around here, and has housed druggies, released prisoners, and God knows who else for years. It is the highest call out area the police need to go to.

I get out of my Audi and grab the pony from out of the boot before locking the car up and flicking the alarm on. I scan the area, searching for anyone who might be loitering about, ready to steal her. My car is mint as fuck and cost me a whack.

But she's also my baby.

Not anymore, my inner brain screams, reminding me of Imogen.

I'm just about to press the buzzer for her door when someone walks out, leaving the door open for me. I head over to the lift, trying not to gag from the stench of stale piss stinking the place out.

I hurry up and get in the lift, and find it's not much better inside. But as long as it gets me to Imogen faster, I don't give a fuck.

I don't like that they live here, though I'm not sure if it's my place to say something. Maybe I can talk Kennedy into coming outside and taking a walk because nothing about this place is healthy. Just inhaling the toxic air around us is making me sick; and my daughter lives here.

Glancing at the apartment numbers so I don't miss her door, I notice Kennedy's flat is next. The door is wide open, and my blood runs cold at the sight that greets me.

The place has been turned upside down, but what has my attention is on the floor. Kennedy is rocking a baby in her arms. She's sitting on the floor, next to a broken table. Her flesh is covered in bruises, and parts of her face are beginning to swell.

"What the fuck happened here?" I yell, stepping into the room.

Kennedy immediately cowers, using her body to shield the baby. The older lady next to her moves to shield them, watching me with fright.

Then Kennedy turns toward me, and the relief on her face has my knees knocking together. She looks at me like I'm her saviour, the answer to all her problems.

"Evan," she breathes.

"I think you need to leave. I've called the police," the lady next to her warns, clearly not knowing who the fuck I am.

Snapping out of her daze, Kennedy butts in. "Mel, this is—"

"Someone who wants to know what the fuck has happened," I finish, taking another step inside.

Her face looked bad when I first walked in, but on closer inspection, it's worse. And from the way she's cradling the baby, I can tell it's more than her face that got hurt.

"Who are you?" Mel demands.

What a loaded question.

"This is Imogen's biological father," Kennedy reveals on a whisper.

I kneel down in front of her, ignoring the glare Mel gives me.

"What happened?" I ask, softening my voice. Kennedy glances down at the baby, like it's the last time she'll ever see her. "Kennedy?"

Heartache like I've never witnessed clouds her expression. Instead of answering, she hands me the baby, leaving me no choice but to take her.

"You have to take her," she chokes out, as Imogen begins to wail.

Fuck, she's got some lungs on her.

I hold her closer, until her head rests on my shoulder, like I've seen Denny do with Hope a million times. I begin to gently pat her bum, and moments later, it's only whimpering coming from her.

I'm a dad!

I hold her a little tighter, and it's in this moment I know I'll never be able to leave her again. Not even for a night. But hell if I know what I'm doing, especially when her mum, so to speak, is hot as fucking hell and is obviously in some kind of abusive relationship.

"I can't just take her," I tell her, wishing she wasn't distracting me from the real issue.

Her wide, frantic gaze meets mine. "You have to. It's the only way to protect her," she announces on a broken sob.

Mel starts rubbing her back affectionately but soon stops when she realises it's only hurting Kennedy more.

"You need to tell me what's happened here. Did your boyfriend hurt you?"

She rears back in disgust. "No. I don't have a boyfriend," she cries, becoming hysterical. "Someone came here. He hurt me. He said my sister owed him three grand. I don't have that kind of money. He said that I'm the insurance she gave him to get his money back if she couldn't. If I don't pay him back, he'll take Imogen and sell her. You have to take her and get her as far away from me as possible."

Mel pulls her into her arms as she breaks, her cries tearing at my heart.

"Tell me exactly what he said," I demand, going into work mode.

She's inconsolable, so Mel tries. "Come on, darlin'. You need to tell him."

Kennedy wipes her tears away, but it's useless as more fall. "That's pretty much it. He told me I've got a month to get him the money. He —" She pauses, staring at Imogen with wonder. "You got her to sleep."

I don't know how. I didn't do anything.

"Calm down. We can sort this," I assure her.

She shakes her head vehemently. "No, we can't. I don't want to lose her, but I have to. She comes first, Evan. She'll always come first, and I can't protect her. Look at me."

"And what about you? Who's going to protect you?" I point out, although I can't deny, her sacrifice is noble.

She glances away. "It doesn't matter."

It does. I don't know why it does, but I know I have to protect her. So I do the only thing I can do. "Get up and go and get yours and Imogen's stuff packed."

Her brows pinch together. "What?"

"Just do it. I need to make a phone call," I tell her, harsher than intended.

"Come on, I'll help you," Melanie offers, helping Kennedy to her feet. I take that moment to look at Kennedy, and I can tell she's in a world of pain. It just makes me want to hunt down this fucker all the more. No one threatens innocent women and children and gets away with it.

What the hell is going on with me?

Once they're out of sight, I glance down at Imogen, seeing her properly for the first time. She has my button nose, the poor thing. I don't know whose colour eyes she has because she's sleeping, but I remember Vicky had dark brown eyes, whereas I have light blue.

She's so tiny, so innocent, curled up on my chest. The thought of someone ever hurting her actually makes me want to do a life sentence in prison for murder.

I dial William's number. I'm going to need help on this one, and my old files. He answers on the third ring.

"'Ello. Miss us already?"

"Jackass, and no. Look, I need a favour."

A loud, booming laugh erupts through the phone, and I have to pull my ear away for a second. "You've been gone a few weeks and already you want a favour."

"Okay, can you just fast track my old files over, please? I need everything we have on the drug bust we did on the Carmack's."

I can't be doing with his banter or teasing digs at the moment. I need answers. I need to know who is doing this and why. The only thing I can come up with is Vicky's past. And that unit was her past.

"What? Why? We closed that case months ago."

Like I need reminding.

"Look, there's a lot I need to explain, but right now, all you need to know is that someone from that case has threatened someone I... Someone close to me," I explain, ignoring that I nearly said someone I care about.

Then I glance down at the little rugrat in my arms, and remember she was threatened too. I'm already in love, and I'll do anything to save her.

"Okay, is there something you need me to do?" he asks without hesitation.

It's the only thing so far that I've missed about my old job. How they have your back. Not that Harris doesn't, it's just that he wants answers first, not later. I suppose we have a lot to figure out before we get to where we need to be.

"Not yet, but I'll keep you posted. Give me an hour, and I'll be home," I tell him before ending the call. I walk towards the hushed voices and into Kennedy's room.

I scan the room, finding it nothing like I pictured a woman's bedroom to be. It's plain, boring, and not a decorative pillow in sight. I expected colour; lots of colour, like my sister's room used to be. But then, I don't really know Kennedy or her tastes yet. She's clearly been struggling if she's living in this shithole.

"Can you take Immy so I can go get her cot and stuff down? I'll call a friend to come and get it all. Unless you want me to buy her new ones?" I ask, not thinking about what Immy might not have.

For all I know, she could just have the basics to get by. I don't even know what a baby needs, though from what I know so far about Kennedy, she doesn't seem like a person who would neglect a child.

"I don't understand what's going on," she admits, standing from the bed. "Are you taking me somewhere? Is Imogen going with you?"

That anguish in her expression cripples me. She doesn't want to part with Imogen, but she would rather suffer and be in danger before anything touches the baby. I admire her for it. And I can see why she is struggling because even I, after only a few minutes, would do anything to make sure she's protected.

I'm also grateful Vicky is dead. She wouldn't sacrifice herself to save her. She wouldn't even hesitate in harming the baby if meant she got what she wanted. She would never have put Imogen first, not like Kennedy is.

"Imogen is staying with you," I assure her.

"No. Look at me," she demands. "Do you think he'll hesitate in doing this to her? You have to take her with you."

"Babe, stop. I'm taking both of you. You're both coming to live with me," I reveal.

I could take her to a friend's or somewhere safe, where they would never think to look for her, but I want them with me, where I know they will be safe.

She shudders, folding her arms over her slim waist. "They'll still find me. And if they find out about you, Imogen will never be safe."

"Do you love her?" I ask, stopping her from continuing.

"With everything in me," she admits.

"Then do what is best for her and stay with her. She needs you," I promise. "Now, can you take Immy so I can go take down her cot or whatever."

"Immy?" she repeats, her nose twitching. "Her name is Imogen."

"Sorry, I guess it just slipped out." I wince, hoping I've not upset her.

"No, it's fine; I like it," she replies.

"So, will you let me help you?" I ask. "Not that I'm going to give you a choice. I will be helping you."

She pulls on the sleeve of her shirt, nodding. "Are you sure? This is a big decision."

I nod, handing Imogen over, and I feel a spark when we touch. I meet her gaze, unable to look away. She isn't a girl who needs saving. I think she could do it herself. So I know that isn't what is drawing me to her. It's something else, something I can't decipher.

I don't want to step on any toes by ordering her about, but I want her with us. I have no clue how to raise a baby, and she seems to be doing a pretty good job of it. I also don't want her to think that's the only reason, so I keep that to myself. I want to use the time to get to know her. I'd like to know how her sister turned out the way she did, but Kennedy didn't.

"Come on, we should change your clothes before you leave," Mel advises, breaking the spell between us.

I step out of the room, realising my mistake. I'm not only taking her in, but I will have to live with her. I'll have to listen to her in the shower, sleep in the next room, and she'll be in my space.

She's beautiful, and if she really is this person, I'm going to find it hard to fight off my attraction towards her.

Calm down, she could have loads of bad habits.

———

An hour later, we're making our way inside my home. I lower Imogen's car seat to the floor and drop the bags next to her. Once I saw the cot and noticed it wasn't new, I decided to leave it where it was. I called Baby Care and ordered everything a baby her age will need. Once I told them our story, they made an exception and will deliver everything today. They even offered to assemble everything, which I'm grateful for. It will give me more time to concentrate on who hurt Kennedy.

I called Harris, letting him know my priorities are elsewhere and explained the situation. He told me to leave as much clothing and stuff in the flat as possible, which I'm glad he reminded me about. We don't want the person coming back and knowing she's moved. It will stall him for a little while, but not by much.

Turning to Kennedy after I drop the keys onto the counter, I notice she's still pretty shaken up.

I startle her when I reach for her hand. "Come on, you need to lie down. I'll get you some ibuprofen too."

She glances at my king-sized bed, before meeting my gaze. "No, I should be awake for when Imogen wakes up," she argues, bringing her shaking hands up to brush her hair from her face.

"I've got Imogen. If you don't want to lie down, at least go run yourself a bath. I have one right down the hall," I declare. "It will help with the pain. Trust me. When you come back out, I'll have a look at those bruises your shirt's been hiding."

"How…"

"I can tell by the way you're walking. When you're out, let me check you over so I know whether I need to take you to the hospital or not."

"But Imogen," she repeats.

"Has me here. Trust me, you'll feel loads better once you are in there."

"Imogen needs a bottle in half an hour, though."

"Stop stalling," I demand, and nudge her in the direction of the bathroom.

Luckily, Denny left some of her things in there, so I show her where everything is and hand her the spare towels.

"Thank you," she murmurs.

I nod, leaving her to sort the rest so I don't do something stupid like offer to clean her up. I head back down the hall, grabbing the car seat and the bag I saw Kennedy pack all the bottles and stuff in.

I get to work unpacking it all, placing it down on the kitchen counter. By the time the bag is empty, my side is covered in so much stuff, I begin to feel overwhelmed.

How hard can making a bottle be?

There's a machine that has bottles, lids, and a bunch of plastic things that look like nipples. I'm stunned into despair, wondering what the fuck is what.

A plastic tub of baby formula sits near the edge, and I reach for it with a triumphant smile, turning it around for instructions.

I can do this.

Twenty minutes later, I'm still no closer to figuring it out. Powdered milk covers my shirt and hands, and I have no fucking clue what to do.

Kennedy emerges from the bathroom and I hear her approaching. I pause with the scoop in my hand, nearly dropping it when she comes into view. She looks hot, seriously hot, and not just because she looks like she's been sitting in a sauna for the past hour.

"Hey," I greet, and gulp when she walks around the breakfast bar in only a baggy T-shirt that barely covers her arse. She has shorts on, but they look more like boxers, and my mind immediately runs through all the dirty things I want to do to her.

Fuck, for a small person, she has pretty amazing legs. I can't help but imagine what they'd feel like wrapped around me.

"Are you okay?" she asks quizzically, then starts to chuckle when she spots the mess I made. "You have baby milk down your shirt."

Damn. I had hoped to have this all sorted by the time she got out. "Yeah, I'm just trying to figure this shit out."

"Here, I'll show you," she offers, her face scrunching up in pain when she moves towards me.

I don't get time to question her because she starts putting together the bottle, and I pay attention, knowing I need to learn.

She flips on the kettle before plugging in the machine and switching it on.

"This is the steriliser. The bottles need to be sterilised after each use to keep them clean. I only make more than one bottle up during the night. I just leave the boiled water in the bottle until she wakes up. Then I add the milk, like so," she explains, then shows me how to put the right amount of powder into the bottle. She's quick and efficient, and I can't take my gaze off her. She makes it look so easy.

When I notice she's not moving anymore, I turn to look at her, finding her staring back at me with a pink blush to her cheeks.

My brows pull together. "What?"

"I said: Where do you keep the jug?"

"Oh, here," I tell her, pointing over her head. I reach up to the cabinet and grab the plastic jug down for her. She fills it with cold water, then plops the bottle with boiling water inside it.

"All done," she finishes, clasping her hands together. "Just let that cool down to lukewarm so it doesn't burn Imogen's mouth, and you're good to go."

"I can do that."

She gives me a blinding smile and we both stand there staring at each other awkwardly. When Imogen breaks the silence by waking up, we snap out of it. We both move to reach for her at the same time. We pause for a split second, but then both of us go to reach for her again.

Shit! Why am I being so awkward?

"Go on, you go. I'll just go... um... lie down. Do you have those painkillers?" she asks timidly, lowering her gaze.

"Yeah, here," I tell her, and walk over to the tablets I'd gotten ready in the mix of making myself look like the milk powder monster.

She takes them from me and swallows them dry. I watch as her throat bobs up and down, and I end up swallowing a gulp myself. My brain thinks of what her throat would look like swallowing something else, but I clear that thought straight away.

Fuck, this is going to kill me.

I quickly grab Imogen out of the car seat and smile down at her. She's so freaking cute. She even has my eyes.

My heart warms, and for once in my life, I feel like I'm right where I need to be. I know for a fact I'm never going to let her down, ever.

In the short amount of time I've known I was a dad, I've managed to move her in and make a bottle by myself. Okay, not by myself, but the thought was there.

"She'll need changing before the bottle's ready. Just make sure you check the temperature."

"How do I check the temperature?" I ask.

"Place a drop on the inside of your wrist. If it's still too hot, pop it back in the jug for a little bit longer."

"Okay."

She slowly leaves, and a part of me wants to call her back, but I know I need to start doing this myself.

I glance at Imogen's clothes, wondering why Kennedy asked me to change her. They seem fine. But then I lift her up and realise she didn't mean her clothes. She was talking about her nappy.

I groan and grab the bag she filled with nappies, along with the changing mat and a bottle, before heading into the living room.

With precise manoeuvring, I manage to lay everything down and lower her onto the mat.

I decide to change her entire outfit into what I'm assuming is a pyjama set, but the task of getting her clothes off becomes impossible.

Whoever the fuck made these vests were *not* thinking of kids when they designed them. At one point, I'm afraid of dislocating her arm while trying to get it out of the sleeve.

"Come on, little one. Help a man out, okay?" I plead, and feel relief when I finally get her stripped down to just her nappy.

To the left, I have baby wipes, nappy bags, and a peg. To the right, I have the nappy and clean baby grow. It's amazing what you pick up from being around your sister. Thank fuck she had a child at eighteen or I'd be fucked right now.

It's not like it's going to be hard, but just in case something does go wrong, I have a spare nappy on standby.

I take in a deep breath before entering what will now be my life.

And I don't mind one single bit.

CHAPTER
SIX

KENNEDY

The bed smells like him. I can't escape his intoxicating scent, and it's nearly driving me crazy. I toss and turn for a second, unable to get comfy, especially when I start to hear Imogen fussing.

I still can't believe he's already so hands on. He hasn't even questioned himself and has taken it all in his stride. I really admire him for it. Most men would use the excuse that they don't know what they're doing to get out of anything and everything, but not Evan. He seems to actually know what he's doing, and what he doesn't know, he's learning.

When I saw him in the doorway back at my flat, I thought my prayers had been answered. If anyone could protect her, it's him, but then he shocked me by moving us in.

I know I'm only an extension to that invitation because of Imogen, but I wasn't going to pass it up, not when it means I get to stay with her.

I close my eyes, hoping sleep finds me, but strings of images from the attack flash in my mind. I feel his grip, the force of his punch, and the unbelievable strength he used to kick me.

If it wasn't for the unimaginable pain I'm still in, I would think it wasn't real. It's like having an out-of-body experience, where it all feels too surreal. I haven't lived with my head in the clouds. I know violence like this exists. I just never believed it would happen to me. I'm a people pleaser and always thought I would never piss someone off enough or get involved with people like that who would hurt me like he did. It was all for nothing. I hate my sister for bringing me into her mess once again. I feel like I'll always be cleaning up after her.

Then there's Evan. I've put his daughter at risk, and after what my sister did to him, he had every right to leave me to fend for myself. But he didn't. Instead, he seems to be handling this better than me.

I fight the tears threatening to fall, knowing they won't fix this or make me feel better.

When Imogen begins to fuss again, I decide to get up and investigate. Although I can't sleep, it still doesn't feel right to lie here, no matter how exhausted I am.

I slowly slide out of bed and walk the short distance to the living room. There, on the floor of the living room, is Evan, with an irritated Imogen wiggling.

I cover my mouth to muffle my giggle when I take him in. He's got a peg pinned to his nose, washing-up gloves on, and is currently dry heaving as he wipes the remains of poop from Imogen's bum.

"Nooooo," he whisper-yells, and I take step forward; worried. Ignoring the pain in my side, I bend forward a little to look closer, and burst out laughing. His head snaps to me and his shoulders slump with defeat. "She just pissed on me."

"She's marking her territory," I tease before trying to make him feel better. "Trust me, it's when she poops in the bath that you have to worry. She's done that to me a few times."

His lips part, and his eyebrows rise to his hairline. "She doesn't?"

"Oh, she does," I confirm.

He holds up the nappy. "How do I get this on?" he grumbles. "When I Google it, it just gives me links to where I can buy them."

Instead of doing it for him, I sit down next to him on the floor and point to the sticky labels at the end of the nappy. "That end always goes under the bum."

He follows my instructions, and in no time has her nappy on. When he reaches for her bed clothes, I question him. "You do know you'll need to dress her again after she has a bath."

"You said to get her changed. I didn't know if you meant nappy or clothes, and because she pooped, I thought I'd do both." He shrugs like it's no big deal.

I go to tell him how thankful I am, when a loud banging noise startles me. I immediately push closer to Evan.

Did the man find me?

Is he here to take Imogen?

A whimper slips past my lips and I cling to Evan when he moves, pulling him back. "Don't answer it," I hiss.

He places Imogen in my arms, giving me no option but to take her, and kneels in front of me. "It's okay. It's a friend from work. He's brought me everything to do with the case involving your sister. Okay?"

My shoulders drop, and I feel stupid. I nod, letting him know I heard.

I don't know much about the case he worked on. Only parts, since· I was the one who picked Vicky up from the police station when she was arrested. She kept calling him a rat and wouldn't stop screaming about him for hours.

Knowing what I know now, I'm surprised he never got her charged with sexual assault. He might not see it that way, but I do. In my eyes, what she did was rape. That said, I don't know what that has to do with what happened today.

Feeling self-conscious, I get up and sit down on the chair. It's as comfy as I imagined the first time I saw it. After grabbing her bottle, I feel bold, so I kick my feet up and tuck Imogen to my chest. I rest my head back against the pillow, relaxing as she begins to drink. It was meant to block out the sounds from outside, but all I hear is him. Feeling safe, the exhaustion pulls me under, and I fall asleep.

———

The throbbing around my injuries stirs me awake. Every inch of me aches, and I know I'm going to be feeling like this for days. I take stock of the room, noticing I'm no longer in the living room. I'm back in Evan's bed, surrounded by his intoxicating scent.

Glancing up at the window, it's dark out, and I groan. I slept the rest of the day away. My stomach rumbles with hunger.

I slide my feet out of the bed, and it hits me. I don't remember walking in here, which means Evan carried me.

My bags are placed in the corner of the room, and I feel guilty for taking up all of his space. I reach for the closest bag, glad when I find a pair of pyjama bottoms. I slide them on, hissing when the band digs into the bruise on my hip bone.

I become lightheaded and grab the edge of the bed for support. Once it subsides, I head out of the room to find Evan. When he's not in the kitchen or living area, I begin to panic.

Rushing back towards the bedroom, I notice a soft glow coming from another room. Walking closer, I hear the hum of a voice.

"We may not have known each other long, but I promise to take care of you. You've got me too now, and I will love you forever," Evan whispers in a soft voice. I've never heard him speak so softly before, and a shiver runs up my spine. "You are already my most favourite person in the entire world."

I step quietly towards the door and peep through the gap. My lips part at everything he has set up already. It's beautiful, and everything I wish I could have given her. A cot lays in one corner with a pink princess canopy. He has a chest of drawers, a changing station, and is currently sitting in a rocking chair, holding a bottle to Imogen's mouth.

He has papers and folders on the table next to him, where there's also a steaming mug of something and a jug of water.

What on earth is all of that? Surely, they can't all be from the case he spoke about.

"Hey, you're awake," he greets, spotting me.

I smile sheepishly, embarrassed he caught me spying. "I'm sorry. I didn't mean to fall asleep on you," I assure him, and step further into the room, mesmerised by everything he's done. "I can't believe I slept through all of this being built. It's beautiful."

"You needed the rest," he states. "Are you hungry, because I ordered a takeout. It's in the microwave. I did try to wake you when it arrived but you were out of it."

Sugar puffs!

My cheeks flame. "Sorry. I'm normally a light sleeper, I promise," I tell him, and glance down at Imogen, who is sucking on her bottle whilst mesmerised by her father. She hasn't looked away from him once. "How has she been?"

"She's been really good. She was a little groggy earlier, but I picked her up and she calmed down," he admits, his voice soft. Seeing her in his arms makes her look even smaller, and she is already a tiny baby. I also can't help but find him more attractive. He looks hot as hell with her in his arms.

Going back to what he said, I let out a sigh. "I'm going to take her back to the doctors," I declare, scared it's more than teething that's bothering her. Her temperature has been up and down, which is beginning to worry me. It's times like this I wish my mum was here to get advice from. It hurts that she's not because she would know exactly what to do.

"What? Why? Did I do something wrong?" he panics, scanning Imogen from head to toe.

"No! No. She's been like this for a week now. She's been so off. She's usually a happy, peaceful baby, but lately she's been so upset; like she's in pain. I took her last Tuesday and they said it's teething, but I don't know," I explain, stroking my finger down her cheek.

Her gaze finally pulls away from Evan, and when she sees me, she flaps her arms in excitement. I laugh along with Evan.

"I think someone's excited to see you," he teases, holding her up.

I take her from him and smile widely at her. She's everything to me. She's my world, and on the days when everything gets to me, she is my reason to keep going. I love her like my own. In fact, the older she gets, the more I've wanted to call myself her mum. A few times it's slipped out, and every time, I've felt guilty because I'm not. She deserves to have one in her life, though, to call someone mum. But now with Evan in the picture—and him being the biological father—I will probably be her aunt from here on out. It's something I want to speak to him about, because I love her and can't picture being anything but a mum to her.

"Let me know when you want to go to the doctors. I'll come with you," he offers, picking up a large file from the pile.

"What's all that?" I ask, and realise how nosey I'm being. We don't know each other well enough yet. "I'm sorry, that was nosey. You don't have to tell me anything."

I look down to find Imogen sleeping soundly on my shoulder, a loud burp escaping her mouth. I chuckle quietly as Evan answers.

"Don't worry about it, it's fine. If you want to pop Immy in the cot, we can talk in the front room." He gets up, taking the stack of files with him, and walks the two steps over to me, kissing Immy on the head. His scent overwhelms my senses and my knees begin to shake. "I'm so glad you found me and told me."

"Why wouldn't I have?"

"Not to speak ill of the dead, but considering your sister's reputation, I'm surprised you weren't concerned I'd be just like her."

"Honestly?"

He smiles. "Of course."

I meet his gaze dead on so he can see I'm telling the truth. I swallow deeply, captivated by his eyes. God, they're beautiful. Shaking my thoughts away, I begin. "At first, I didn't want to find you. I wondered about everything going on in your life, and if you were still doing the job that you do. I didn't want Imogen getting caught up in that. I've seen *Die Hard* and other movies when their kids get used for revenge. But I realised I was just making excuses. I guess in the end, I just wanted what was best for her. I imagined what my life would be like without her and it killed me. And that's what it would have been like for you. I know you didn't know about her, but she's special. I knew the minute you did, you would fall in love with her. How could you not?" I murmur. "She's a fighter, and she deserves the very best of everything. That includes you."

He's taken by surprise by my words. "Wow! Didn't expect you to be *that* honest."

"I just don't want secrets between us. We've got to get along for Imogen," I reply, before taking a plunge. "We do need to talk about things. And get to know each other."

"We'll get there, I promise. But first, let's get Immy to bed and talk about what happened this morning, okay?" he says, bumping my chin with his fist.

I've never had anyone give me what he's giving me right now. What happened this morning has honestly scared the loving poop out of me. I don't want to be one of those scared women, but I know if it hadn't been for Evan taking us in, I would still be at home, scared to my wits end and struggling over what to do.

"Okay," I agree and take Imogen over to the cot. I lay her down in the new comfy bed and wrap her up, but not too much in case she overheats. The nights are getting colder as of late, but thankfully, Evan can afford to have his heating on, unlike me. It's not a luxury I'm used to having.

It's another reason it's going to kill me when it's time for me to finally leave here. I can't give her what he can.

In just a day, he's bought her everything I wished I could have.

I don't want to leave her, but after seeing all he's done, I can't help but wonder if she's better off without me.

CHAPTER
SEVEN

EVAN

I have to get out of the small room. Having her so close has the walls closing in on me. It didn't help that when I carried her to bed, I got to feel what it was like to have her in my arms. Then I got a glimpse of her body, and I felt like a creeper when I reacted to it. Until I caught a glimpse of the marks that fucker left on her flesh. I had to go out into the garden and punch the fuck out of the punching bag.

There is nothing I hate more than a man who hurts women or kids. It's weak and cowardly, and I'd love to take them each on to show them how a real man fights. Whoever hurt her didn't hold back, and it makes me sick to my stomach that he went that far to get a point across. She is a tiny, delicate woman, and she had no chance of defending herself.

No woman has ever affected me like this before.

I'm glad she was dead to the world when I carried her in because if she had looked at me with those doe eyes, I wouldn't have been able to control myself.

I even watched her for a moment, because I got to really look at her. She's naturally beautiful, but when she sleeps, she looks peaceful. It makes her beauty shine.

Walking into the kitchen, I take the containers out of the microwave and place them on the side. Getting a couple of fresh plates out, I start grabbing some stuff for myself when Kennedy appears.

"Smells yummy."

See? So fucking cute.

"I ordered it an hour or so ago, so take what you want and I'll warm it up for you."

"What time is it?" she questions, scanning the room for a clock.

"It's just gone eleven," I answer.

"Oh gosh! I can't believe I slept that long," she stresses, whilst grabbing food.

I'm actually surprised she's throwing food on her plate the way she is. She doesn't seem like the type of person who would stuff her face in front of a male. Then again, we aren't dating, and I'm probably being judgemental. But since every girl I've dated has eaten like they're worried someone will notice, it's no wonder I jumped to conclusions.

I'm actually glad that she isn't like them.

"Like I said, you must have needed it," I tell her, smiling.

Walking into the front room after heating up our food, Kennedy follows me.

"I just feel bad. I mean, I left Imogen with you and you've only just met each other. Then I crash in your bed like I own the place. It just doesn't feel right. Me being here and all."

"I wouldn't have offered if I didn't mean it, Kennedy. I want to help you, and being here will help keep you safe. I'm not going to let you get hurt," I explain, then add. "Again."

In fact, having her here feels right somehow, and not just because of Imogen either. Something about seeing her in my bed, sleeping, did something to me. But I know with everything going on, if I start something with her, it will most likely end badly.

"Thank you," she whispers, and I get the sense she doesn't receive help very often.

"What do you do for a living?" I ask, wanting to get to know her.

Once she's done chewing, she replies, "I work in a cafe in town. I'm hoping to get something better, but there aren't many jobs available right now."

She's cute when she rambles.

"How long have you been working there?"

"Four years," she answers. "What about you? How long have you been working for the police?"

"I'm not working for them now," I correct. "I've actually started my own business with a good friend of mine, Harris."

"Sounds interesting. What will you be doing now?" she asks, taking another bite from her food.

"A bit of everything, I guess. We will be fitting security systems for people, doing private investigations and security for people who hire us. It will vary. We'll probably still have to look into cheating spouses, but it will get better."

"Sounds really good," she murmurs, and hesitates for a second before continuing. "If you don't mind me asking, what happened with my sister? The night—you know—Imogen was conceived. Even though I know she was a b-i-t-c-h, I never thought she'd be capable of that."

My lips twitch when she spells out the word bitch. But come to think of it, I don't think I've heard her swear.

Finished with my food, I put my plate to the side and give her my full attention. "I'm not really supposed to talk about the case or anything involved with it; but because no harm can really come of it, I'll tell you. Your sister was mixed up with some pretty shitty people. I had been undercover for a year. Your sister always came on to me, but I pushed her away every time. And before you ask, it wasn't because I was on a job; it was because I didn't like your sister. I know that's wrong since she's your sister and all, but..."

"I understand. You don't need to apologise to me. She has never been a nice person, so whatever you have to say, I can take it. I've probably heard worse."

I give her a gentle smile and store that information in the back of my mind for later. I want to know how the two of them could be complete opposites.

"Well, she basically sold herself to the men if they offered, and slept with the ones she thought she could get something out of. She hung around the unit more than any of the men who worked there.

"I guess on the last night—before the whole raid happened—she thought she would slip me something, though I could never prove that. I hadn't drunk anything until that night. I wanted to keep a level head, but my boss said I needed to make sure I blended in, that I needed to be relaxed.

"I started to feel light-headed, and my vision began to blur. I knew something was wrong, but the next thing I knew, I woke up naked in one of the bunks at the back of the unit with your sister next to me. Every day afterwards, I would remember something else about that night; about her," I admit, keeping my voice indifferent.

I don't want her to know how much it bothers me knowing my dick was inside her skanky sister.

"Oh my gosh," she breathes, her eyes pooling with unshed tears. "I can't believe her."

"It is what it is."

"And you knew nothing about the pregnancy?"

"Like I said the day we met, I knew nothing. I didn't exactly keep in touch with everyone after. My part of the job was done. The rest was down to the courts and prosecutors."

"She told me you knew," she states, something she's already told me.

"No. If I had known, I would have taken Imogen far, far away from her," I promise. "I know you explained some things already the day you first came here, but can you explain how Immy came to be in your care? Some things are still fuzzy from that day, and I don't remember everything you said."

"Vicky left the night she gave birth," she reveals.

"That soon?" I ask, not surprised, but still, I thought women needed time to recover.

"Yeah. She didn't care. After a week went by, the hospital helped me get parental guardianship of Imogen so I could grant permission for the tests and procedures they needed to do. I found Vicky and got her to sign away her rights to me. She couldn't do it quick enough. Then when she died, I got granted full custody."

"How are you two totally different?" I blurt out, enjoying the flush to her cheeks.

"I don't know," she replies quietly. "She's always been the way she is. Even as a kid. I'm the youngest. My brother—who died from cot death when he was six months old—would have been the eldest. Vicky was the middle child, and my mum used it as an excuse for her behaviour. But I knew it wasn't because of that. There was something dark inside Vicky, something she didn't want to control, but something she gave her control to. She was always getting into trouble, even before our parents died. It got worse after though."

"What happened after?"

"We were separated for a while, and she acted out because of it. But then social services found us a home who were willing to take us both in, and she ruined it. They separated us again, and put me in the care of a good family. They agreed to still let me see her; I just couldn't live with her, and she resented me for that. Or at least, that's how it felt," she reveals. "She tried so hard to get me kicked out. She stole my foster dad's car. She stole money. And it was wearing on them. I could sense it."

"Did they kick you out?"

"Thankfully, no, but it did stop them from forming a bond with me. I just felt like a guest there, and not part of a family."

I knew her sister was a bitch, but Jesus... This is something else. "And there was never a time when you did get along?"

I knew Vicky had a hard past and that her parents died. I also knew she had a sister, but because she never popped up on our database, no one ever pursued it.

"Not that I remember. She'd take everything my parents ever

bought me. Whether it was a pair of knickers that would never have fitted her, she'd take them. She caused arguments, fights, and never cared who she was hurting." She glances away, biting her lip. "She'd bully me non-stop, and I took it because she was my sister. I loved her; or I did at one point before she completely ruined it. I kept hoping she would change, but then after Imogen, I couldn't keep making excuses for her anymore."

I hate that the only family she had left was a bitch. She must have grown up lonely.

At least now she has me and Imogen.

Fuck! Where the hell did that come from? Needing a drink, I get up quickly, startling her. "I'm going to get a beer. Do you want one or do you want something else?"

"Thank you. If you don't mind, I'll have tea, or water if you don't have any," she replies.

I take her empty plate and head into the kitchen. I take my time making her cup of tea, needing a moment to gather myself.

We might not have had the same upbringing, but I know what it's like to be in an environment with a toxic person. Vivian was just like Vicky. Both were cruel and selfish, only caring about what they wanted or needed.

W alking back in, I hand Kennedy her tea and sit down on the sofa next to her. Kennedy has made herself at home, which I find I like. It means she's comfortable with me, with us. She has her feet tucked up, and has snuggled a pillow to her chest.

"So," I start, and reach over to grab a file. "I've been going through these files all night, and so far, nothing stands out. There's no mention of who Vicky could owe since she was just a small fish in a big pond. But I do have this, which has pictures of everyone connected to the case." Her gaze is immediately drawn to the folder, her lower lip trembling. "Do you think you can look through them and see if you recognise him?"

She nods her head firmly, but with the way her hands shake as she takes it, I begin to doubt my decision. She just went through a traumatic ordeal and needs time to recover. But since now is the best time to do it, we can't wait.

"I can do that," she agrees, opening the folder to the first page.

I keep an eye on her as she flicks through, ready to stop if it becomes too much. "Are you doing okay? Not just with this but with what happened."

"I guess. Everything seems to have happened so quickly. I ache in places I didn't know I could ache. My entire body feels swollen and sore," she reveals, shrugging. "But other than the fact I don't understand what is going on, I'm doing okay."

"I promise I won't let him touch you again," I tell her fiercely, needing her to hear the truth in my words.

She looks up from the folder and holds my gaze. "I know you won't."

The conviction in her tone has my pulse racing. She's put all her trust and faith in me and has done so willingly. She doesn't really know me, so the fact she has, I can't help but feel a sense of pride.

Now I need to live up to my word and make sure nothing happens to her again. I don't think I'll be able to live with myself if it does.

Not knowing what else to say, I let her flick through the folder in silence. Meanwhile, I keep myself busy and flick through tonight's highlights of the game that I missed.

Half an hour later, Kennedy whimpers. I shoot my gaze to her, finding tears slipping down her cheeks. Her eyes are filled with fear, and her fingers tremble around the folder.

"Have you found him?" I ask. When she doesn't pull her gaze away from the page, I slide off the sofa and kneel in front of her. I pry the folder from her hands and keep a hold of them. "Look at me."

"It's him," she whispers, and gently removes her hand from mine, pointing down to the picture. I take the folder and glance at the picture she gestured to, feeling my blood run cold.

"Fuck!"

"What?" she stresses.

I sit back on my heels and run my fingers through my hair.

Drake fucking White. One of the biggest, most ruthless drug suppliers in town. No one has ever been able to get that fucker charged with anything. Even with the evidence we've stacked against him, he still manages to get free.

"Tell me! You're scaring me," Kennedy pleads, and I snap my gaze up to hers. Seeing her so scared has me wanting to pull her into my arms.

"Are you sure this is him?" I ask quietly.

"Yes. I'll never forget those eyes or that scar," she tells me. Her body is shaking uncontrollably and she's starting to become hysterical.

"Look, everything is going to be okay. But this guy... this guy is seriously bad news. Whatever your sister was mixed up in with him, it was bad. He's not known to give second chances. He also demands having a backup plan for people who buy off him."

"That's why he threatened me to pay up or he'd take Imogen," she hiccups, tears falling down her face. I wipe them away, but they keep on flowing. Seeing her like this is breaking my heart.

"Babe, he won't touch you again," I assure her. I grab my phone off the table and dial William's number.

"You'd better have a reason for interrupting my television time," he growls, and any other time, I'd tease him about it, but this is serious.

"I need that help you promised me," I demand, my tone leaving no room for argument.

"Fuck! Who is it?"

"Drake White."

"Shit!"

He's got that right.

But unlike before, Drake White isn't going to get away with it this time.

I won't stop until he's dead or behind bars.

He has no idea who he has messed with.

CHAPTER EIGHT

KENNEDY

After listening to Evan talk to his boss, and witnessing his concern, I did nothing but toss and turn last night. I barely got any sleep. Every time I shut my eyes, I either saw Drake or the fear Evan let creep into his expression.

The way he tried to comfort me last night still flashes through my mind. I can still feel his soft touch as he wiped my tears away and held my hands. I can hear the gentleness in his tone as he assured me everything would be okay.

But nothing about this is okay.

He said this Drake guy is the worst of the worst, and he's coming for me.

I'm not looking forward to today. I don't know what's going to happen. They put a warrant out for his arrest, but I have a sinking feeling things are about to get a lot worse.

There were no witnesses to my attack, so even if they do arrest him, his lawyer will have him out in no time. I mentioned it to Evan, and he explained he wanted to spook Drake. He thinks letting him know they are watching him will get him to back off, or at least until they pin something solid on him.

Personally, I don't think Evan believes what he's saying to me. He couldn't even look me in the eye when he said it.

After feeding Imogen and getting her dressed, I put her in her Bumbo activity floor seat so I can go and clean up the kitchen. I made a mess making Evan breakfast, but I had to do something to thank him for letting us stay.

I feel bad that he had to sleep on the sofa. I did offer to sleep there, but he was having none of it. I even pointed out it would be like a bed to me with how small I am, but he declined my offer.

A knock at the door startles me from what I'm doing. I drop the dishcloth and move to the hall to see if Evan heard.

After he ate, he went to take a shower and get dressed. Still hearing the shower, I walk towards the door, hoping it's just a delivery.

A beautiful woman is standing on the other side, and I recognise her as the one I saw when I first came to visit.

"Hey, um, i-is Evan here?" she asks, her complexion paling.

She's surprised to see me, and I panic, wondering if she's his girlfriend. We've not spoken about that, and I should have asked if it would be a problem.

I tense when I realise Imogen is in the room behind me. If this woman doesn't know who I am, she might not know about Imogen.

Will she go crazy?

"Yes, he's..." I trail off, wondering how I can word it without it sounding bad if she is his girlfriend. "He's actually in the shower. Would you like to come in and wait?"

Before she answers, Imogen starts to cry, and forgetting the woman, I rush over to her, lifting her out of her Bumbo seat.

I turn back to the woman, about to offer her a seat, but she's watching me, sadness lurking in her eyes as she stops just inside the door.

"If he's busy, I can come back," she offers, unable to meet my gaze.

Have I made things awkward?

Sugar! Did they break up over Imogen?

"He'll be out—"

"Oh, hey, Lexi. I thought I heard the door," Evan greets, and I turn to him, relief filling me.

He can sort—Holy Moley.

I nearly choke on my saliva as he stands there, wet, tanned and tattooed. He's only wearing a towel, giving me a full view of his chest. He has a tribal tattoo that runs across his chest and along his ribs. He also has a dragon tattoo that covers the top part of his arm.

Holy Moley, he's hot.

How did I miss this?

I clench my thighs together as I follow the lines of his sculpted, drool-worthy abs. Each muscle is defined by deep ridges, and I yearn to run my fingers down them.

He catches me staring, and his pupils dilate. I spin around to avoid his intense stare, rocking a crying Imogen in my arms.

"I wanted to talk to you, but I can see this is a bad time," Lexi declares, before turning to leave.

"Wait," Evan calls. "Let me just go get some clothes on and we'll talk."

He quickly rushes from the room, not letting her reply. He seems to do that a lot, or has since I've known him.

I turn to Lexi, feeling awkward. "I'm Kennedy," I introduce myself, manoeuvring Imogen to my other arm so I can reach out to shake her hand.

"I'm Lexi," she states, forcing a smile.

I can't quite grasp what her relationship to Evan is. She seems uncomfortable by my presence, but isn't exactly acting like a girlfriend, or an ex for that matter.

She seems nice and isn't acting standoffish, which is why I'm struggling to understand what is going on.

Evan walks back into the room, now dressed in dark jeans and a short-sleeved black T-shirt. "Would you like a drink?" he offers.

"NO!" Lexi blurts out, then lowers her voice. "Sorry. No. I can't stay long."

Evan holds his hands out for Imogen and I hand her over, smiling. He's so hands on and already adapting to his new role.

"Okay. I'd like you to meet someone. This is Kennedy," he begins, pointing to me.

"We've met," she replies, forcing a smile.

"And this little pumpkin is Immy—short for Imogen. She's my daughter," he announces, puffing his chest out.

He's so busy gazing down at a fussing Imogen that he doesn't notice the way Lexi's expression falls.

She didn't know.

I want to reach out and comfort her, but something about her body language and expression has me staying out of her business.

"*Daughter?*" she repeats, the word bitter on her tongue. Her eyes bug out as she closes her arms over her slim frame.

Evan glances up at her tone, his brow furrowed. "Yes, daughter," he confirms, a bite to his tone.

"Oh, fuck! I forgot I have a doctor's appointment. I'd best be going before I'm late," she rushes out.

I hold back a retort, wanting to call her out for swearing around Imogen. I'm not a fan of swearing anyway. It's judgemental, but I find it trashy. It's a pet peeve of mine, but it only really gets to me when people do it around children.

I watch as Evan opens his mouth and moves towards her, but Lexi is out of the door before he can take another step. I watch like a deer caught in headlights, and wonder what I should do.

"Do you want me to take Imogen so you can go after her?" I ask quietly, feeling bad it's mine and Imogen's presence that has caused this.

"Why?"

He should already know why. It doesn't take a genius to work out what was going on with her.

"Because I don't want you two to break up," I start, but Evan's laughter interrupts me. "What?" I frown, not liking the fact he's laughing at me.

"You think we're together?" he asks, his lips twitching.

"Well, she's clearly in love with you. When I opened the door, she looked like her whole world had fallen apart at the sight of me. And she couldn't leave quick enough. I don't buy the doctor excuse."

"Look, I know she was lying about the doctor's appointment. I just don't know why. But I can assure you that we have never been together."

"Why do I have a feeling there's a *but*?" I murmur, then lower my gaze to the floor, my cheeks heating. "I'm sorry, it's none of my business."

He reaches over, lifting my chin with his knuckle. His eyes soften in the corners as he steps a little closer. "You're going to be in my life for a long time, Kennedy. You deserve to know."

"Okay," I whisper, trying to ignore the way his words are doing crazy things to my insides right now.

"I thought we had a thing a while back, but it was nothing. In fact, *she* turned *me* down."

"But you're hot!" I blurt, outraged. I slap my forehead, groaning. I need a flipping filter.

Why do I always do this to myself?

And why does he have to be so good looking? It makes me verbal vomit when I'm around him because I'm so on edge.

"Thanks, so are you," he teases with a wink, which has my cheeks burning more. "It took me a while to realise that it would never have worked out between us. I was hoping for something that wasn't there between us."

"What do you mean?" I ask curiously, grinning when I see Imogen lying down on Evan's shoulder, her mouth hanging open in an O shape as she sleeps.

"I want to settle down," he admits. "A lot happened last year with my sister. She was not only pregnant, but she also got engaged, and I realised what I had been missing."

He tries to shrug it off as nothing, but I can see it matters to him. I can see it's what he really wants.

"You sure it's not some sibling rivalry?" I lightly retort.

He chuckles, the sound sending shivers up my spine. "No. I love my sister and would give her the world if I could because she deserves it. But seeing it there, right in front of me, it just hit me. I wanted to be settled down in a family home, and not some three-bed bungalow. And someday have it filled with kids."

"You got one of those," I remind him, smiling at a snoring Imogen.

"Yeah, I do, don't I," he agrees, beaming, but when he meets my gaze, there's a heat there, and I have to clench my thighs together.

"So... um... was there something you needed to do today before you have to be at the police station?" I ask.

My stomach turns at the reminder. I've felt sick ever since he announced he will be leaving us when they do arrest Drake. He assured me it was only to make sure they have the right guy, and to gauge Drake's reaction over it. Luckily, his old boss is okay with him doing that as long as he doesn't cause a scene.

"Funny you should ask that. After what happened with my sister last year, she put distance between us. She's not fallen out with me as such, but she needed time to process my part in it all," he begins. "Her boyfriend just text me to tell me she's over her snit, and to come over whenever to visit. Now that I know Immy is really mine, I was wondering if we could go see her. I want her to be the first person to meet Imogen."

I pause for a second, thinking about it. I've never really left Imogen with anyone other than the nursery staff, and on the odd occasion, Melanie. Sucking it up, I give Evan a smile.

"Sure. I'll do some washing and cleaning whilst you are gone. It's the least I can do for you letting us stay."

"Kennedy, you are misunderstanding me; I want you to come as well."

"To meet your sister?" I ask, my voice high-pitched.

"Yes," he confirms, laughing at my reaction.

I glare. "I can't meet your sister. She might hate me or get the wrong idea. My sister was a... you know; and your sister might think I'm a... you know, too."

"No one would ever accuse you of being a bitch," he responds softly.

My shoulders sag with relief. I've been so scared he'll label me the same as Vicky.

But meeting his family? It's not exactly high on my list of things to do. Ever. Because once people hear about where I come from, who I'm related to… they judge me. They judge me for what my sister has done, and as soon as Denny finds out what my sister did to her brother, she's going to hate me. There's no way that she won't.

That said, I know seeing her is important to him, and I don't want to risk him staying in because I refuse to go.

"Okay… But don't leave me," I plead, not wanting to be left alone.

I don't know anything about her or his family. I'm not the best at socialising, which is why my best friend is twenty-six years my senior. I don't have anything in common with people my age.

What if she asks me to leave?

What if she hits me?

Jeeze Louise, it's his sister. How bad could she be?

CHAPTER
NINE

EVAN

I'm nervous as fuck as I knock on my sister's door—which is unlike me. I never got like this the day she went missing and I showed up unannounced. It's always been my job to stay calm and alert.

I think it's different this time because I don't just want her approval. I need it. I need us to form a relationship that we never got to do when we were kids.

I don't think she'll disapprove of the baby, but she will when she finds out about Vicky and how it came to be. After all, she's just gone through something similar with her friend.

I also need her to accept Kennedy, and make them both feel welcome.

Mason pulls open the door, not surprised to see it's me. "Alright, mate. She's just getting Hope dressed," he explains, before his gaze falls on Kennedy. His eyebrows rise, but once he spots Imogen in the car seat, his head snaps up to me.

I can see myself in Imogen now, so I know he can too. I just hope he doesn't say anything to Denny before I can.

"Are we okay to come in?" I ask when he just stands there.

He shakes out of his daze, pulling the door open wider. "Yeah, um, come in."

We follow him into the front room, where I lower the car seat down by the single armchair, signalling to Kennedy to sit down. She's been strangely quiet from the moment I told her she was coming with us.

She isn't good at hiding her emotions, so I know she's nervous to meet Denny. She isn't the one who should be worried. It should be me.

It didn't feel right letting the family meet Imogen and not her. She belongs at our side, and I want them to like her too.

Footsteps on the stairs have me standing back up from the arm of the sofa. When Denny walks in, she looks surprised to see me, but more surprised and curious as to who Kennedy is. I guess I didn't tell her to expect me today.

She gives Imogen a quick glance, and I ignore the pang of disappointment in my chest at her not seeing Imogen is mine the same way Mason did.

"Hey," she greets, handing a happy Hope over to Mason.

"Hey, sis," I greet back, then move forward to wrap her up in a hug. "I'm sorry, for everything."

She squeezes her arms around me. "It's not your fault. I was just too stubborn to see past that."

I shake my head, ready to argue, but then her head tilts in Kennedy's direction.

Shit. Here it goes.

"This is Kennedy, and this little one is Imogen—my daughter."

She doesn't say anything for a second, and I start to worry. My sister has an opinion on everything and anything.

Hurt flashes across her features. "Excuse me?"

"I didn't know about her—not until a month ago. We were waiting for the DNA results to come back. And now here we are," I explain in a rush.

"DNA results? I don't understand. How did this happen?"

Mason coughs into his hand. "I'm pretty certain you should know that."

I glare in his direction. "Really?"

He grimaces, about to reply, but then Denny continues. "But I didn't think you were seeing anyone. You said you didn't have time and that's why..."

She stops and leans into Mason, her expression crumbling. She was going to say that's why I wasn't there for her.

I hate that I made her feel like her time wasn't important. I told her the truth. My job did take up all of my time. I didn't have time for family or to meet someone—which I regret now more than anything. I also didn't disclose what my job entailed or what they asked from me. I thought it would sound like an excuse to her.

Still, I hate that I've hurt her again. I rub my hand down my face, knowing I need to explain. I just wish I didn't have to. "It's a long story. I was drugged and taken advantage of. I didn't find out about Imogen until a month ago."

"Are you fucking kidding me?" she snaps, her attention zoning in on Kennedy. "Get out! Get out of my house!"

"Denny!" I snap, utterly shocked by her outburst.

"You bring a slut into my house, near my kid, and you think I'd be okay with it," she retorts.

Kennedy's tears fall down her cheeks, and she stands, visibly shaking. I stand between them in case Denny goes for her.

"It's okay. I can leave," Kennedy assures her, her words breaking.

What?

No.

I turn, pulling her into my arms. She tries to push me off, but I refuse to let go. I narrow my gaze on Denny. "Watch your mouth, Denny," I snap, as Mason lowers Hope into her bouncy chair, strapping her in.

Denny's gaze goes from me to Kennedy, her lip curling. "Are you serious right now, Evan? She raped you. She assaulted you and kept your baby away from you."

"Denny, Kennedy isn't Imogen's biological mother," I begin,

cursing to myself. "Imogen's biological mum abandoned her the day she gave birth, and left her in Kennedy's care. She's her mum in every sense of the word, but if you want technical answers, she's actually her aunt."

Denny pauses, tears filling her own eyes. "What?"

"She's not the person who did what you're accusing," I state, not wanting to use the term rape.

She throws her hand up, covering her mouth. Her gaze widens further. "You just let me speak to her like that," she accuses.

"I didn't think. Fucking hell, I'm nervous as fuck here. It's not every day you find out you're a dad and then move the mum and kid in," I point out, brushing my fingers through my hair.

Although, it does feel good to finally get all of this shit out.

"You moved her in?" Denny breathes, but her eyes narrow at the last minute. "Wait, are you sure about all of this? How do you know she's not using you?"

Her attitude is starting to piss me off. "You're seriously going to go there? As I recall, you and Mason didn't have the best start either. At least when Kennedy found me, she didn't mess around to tell me I'm Imogen's dad," I snap, feeling my blood boil.

How dare she?

Her eyes go wide. Mason steps forward, his posture rigid, itching to fight. "I think you should go," he growls, and my eyes narrow on his.

"Don't worry, I am," I seethe, then address Denny. "I wanted you to be the first to know, and the first to meet her. I see I shouldn't have fucking bothered. Out of everyone, I never expected you to react like this. If you can't accept Kennedy and Imogen into your life, or into mine, then I don't want to know you. You can be the one to explain to Hope why she doesn't see her cousin and her uncle."

I grab the car seat before taking Kennedy's hand. I don't stop to console Denny when I hear her cry, or bother to address the remark Mason barks at me.

I keep walking

"Hey, mate," one of Mason's brothers calls as he walks towards us.

When he sees my facial expression, he frowns, but doesn't say anything further. I'm glad he doesn't because I'm ready to blow a fuse. After getting Imogen strapped into the car, I move around to the passenger side of the car, opening the door for Kennedy. Once she's in, I start to buckle her in like a dickhead, but her hand reaches for mine, stopping me.

My gaze meets her big brown doe eyes that are filled with sadness. She's struggling to keep it together.

Unable to prevent what I'm about to do, my hands reach out to her cheeks, my thumbs running lightly under her eyes as the first of her tears fall. We stare into each other's eyes, neither one of us able to find the strength to look away. The dead silence in the air becomes too much, and I find myself blinking, moving my hands away from her face.

Whatever just passed between us is something neither one of us is ready for.

Driving in silence starts to get to me after five minutes. I'm about to break the silence when Kennedy's sweet, small voice carries across the car.

"I'm sorry, so sorry," she chokes out, breaking out into a sob.

I reach across the console, grabbing her hand in mine. Her skin is cold under my warm touch, and I see her shiver from the corner of my eye. My mind drifts back to her words, wondering what she's sorry for. She didn't do anything. I did. I shouldn't have taken either of them. I should have spoken to Denny on my own first, and explained everything. I shouldn't have unloaded it all like that.

"No, I'm the one who is sorry. I didn't know she would be that judgemental. I should have explained over the phone or gone on my own to see her first. I shouldn't have subjected you to that kind of behaviour," I declare. "I swear, if I knew she would do that, I wouldn't have taken either of you."

"I don't want you to fall out with your family," she whispers. "Not over me; not over what my sister did. Imogen doesn't deserve it."

"Hey." I squeeze her hand in mine. "You're right. Imogen doesn't deserve this; she deserves a family who accept her for who she is, and not where she came from or how she was conceived. As much as I hate what Vicky did, I have Imogen. *I have you*," I rasp, the last words barely a whisper.

Her intake of breath tells me she heard me, but I can't find it in me to care. I want her to know. Because it's true.

There is just something about Kennedy that has me feeling over-protective—that wants to get to know her. It's not because she's hot as fuck either. It's the way she loves and adores Imogen. It's the way she willingly put Imogen first, even though it meant she'd be in danger. She's also incredibly sweet. She doesn't swear, and the way she looks at me... Fuck! Just remembering the way she looked at me when I walked out in just a towel this morning makes my dick twitch. I wanted to bend her over the sofa and take her right there.

"I know. I just feel like this is my fault somehow. But then, no matter how I look at it, I'd have always turned up at your door and told you about Imogen."

"And you'll never truly understand how thankful I am to you for that; or how lucky I feel that you are who you are."

Kennedy laughs, catching me off guard, and I can't help but smile whilst listening to her. It's the first time I've seen her laugh, and her face... God, she's fucking beautiful.

"So, what you are saying is: you're glad I'm not like my sister."

"There is that too," I agree through laughter. "But seriously, I'm just glad it's you who will be the mother to my child."

I park outside home and slide out of the car, leaving Kennedy speechless. I head around the car to the passenger side as Lexi walks out of her house with the same date I saw her with the last time. When she spots me, she gives me a small smile before laughing loudly at something her date says. I ignore them and open Kennedy's door, kneeling down to talk to her.

"Are you okay?"

"You want me to be her mother?" she asks, her breath hitching.

"No, baby," I reply, watching her expression. "You already are her mother."

She lets out a sob before throwing herself into my arms. Thank fuck she thought to unclip her belt, otherwise she would have jarred her injuries.

She clings to my T-shirt, her tears soaking through the material. I rub her back and assure her everything is going to be okay. When she pulls back, her face is a breath away from mine.

Everything freezes around us, and it's just us in the moment. I lean in a touch to gauge her reaction. When she doesn't move away, I take that as my cue and press my lips to hers. They're soft, full, and I can't get enough. It's when I feel her tongue run along my bottom lip that everything in that moment switches, and instead of the slow, soft kiss, it becomes heated and aggressive. I can't hold her close enough. She moans into my mouth, and the zipper of my jeans digs into my erection.

A loud cry fills the car and snaps us both out of our embrace. The lust and desire evaporate a little.

We turn our heads slightly to Imogen. I forgot for a minute that she was with us. I open my mouth, but I don't know what to say. Kennedy's lost some colour to her cheeks, but my gaze is drawn to her lips, which are fuller from our kiss. Her tears have now dried, but her eyes still shine with them.

She's beautiful.

I get to my feet, rubbing the back of my neck. "I'll get Immy," I offer.

I inwardly groan at how stupid I sound. I'm a grown-ass man who has no trouble talking to a room full of people, making new friends, or any of that bullshit. I've never had a problem with women either, but with Kennedy, it's all new. Including the feelings she evokes inside of me.

She nods, and I move to the back, where I pull the door open. Imogen has her ears in a tight grip, wailing.

"Shit," I hiss, pulling her hands down.

"What's wrong?" Kennedy asks, rushing to my side.

I lean away to give her room to see. "She was doing that this morning too," I caution.

She brushes past me as she leans in to unbuckle her. "Yeah, the doctors said she's teething. Everything I've read on it says the same thing, but it still worries me."

"Here, I've got her," I declare.

"I've got her," she assures me, stepping back.

My hand goes to her hip, steadying her, and I glance down at Imogen over Kennedy's shoulders. "Her ears look sore."

After a second or two of enjoying her pressed against me, Imogen once again starts to cry. We both move to the left to let each other past, only we end up bumping into each other. We do the same again, only this time, we both move to the right. Chuckling, I grab a hold of Kennedy's hips and pick her up, turning and placing her down behind me like she weighs nothing. Her eyes are wide, filled with desire, and her luscious mouth parts.

I grab Imogen's changing bag from the back of the car, before locking up and walking towards the house. Kennedy already has the spare key ready and is opening the door when I get there.

I watch her arse swing side to side in her tight jeans and will myself not to get another hard-on with my daughter in the room. I only hope I can make it through another night with her in the room next to me without pouncing on her. I want to make her mine in every single way. Now that I've had a taste, my body is already craving more of her.

The minute the door shuts behind me, my phone starts ringing in my back pocket. Grabbing it, I look at the screen and groan.

She couldn't keep her mouth shut.

"Hey, Nan," I answer, unable to hide my discomfort.

"You got something to tell me, young man?"

"I cannot believe she had the nerve to call you. I wanted to tell you myself."

"She called me in absolute tears. Now, I want to hear it from you," she demands sternly, not a tone I'm used to my nan using with me.

"Long story short, on my last job—before Denny's case—I was drugged and a woman had sex with me whilst I was unconscious. Just over a month ago, the sister of the same woman knocked on my door to me tell me about Imogen—my five-month-old baby. I didn't believe it at first, but she came with a DNA test. We sent it off and bam, the baby's mine. They're both living with me, and the biological mum is dead," I rush out, hating that I'm repeating myself.

I've still got my dad to tell, but I know Denny has probably called him by now too. The thought angers me. She knew I would want to tell the others, but after her reaction, I was going to put it off until she calmed down.

"Oh my, sweetie. You were raped," she gasps, and I hear tears in her voice.

"No, Nan. I don't look at it like that. Yes, I was taken advantage of, but I don't feel like a victim," I assure her, keeping my gaze on Kennedy.

She gives me a small smile before settling down on the sofa with Imogen and a fresh bottle. I feel like shit that she's the one feeding her. She needs a break. She still looks tired, worn, and sore as fuck from the attack—even after sleeping most of the day yesterday.

"Are you listening to me?" Nan snaps, causing my body to jolt.

"Sorry, I, um… look, I need to go. I have another call," I lie.

"I wasn't born yesterday. I'm coming around in the week, and before you think of making more excuses, I'll do it when you're least expecting me," she warns.

And she means every word. I wouldn't put it past her to turn up at five in the morning when she knows we'll definitely be in.

"Consider me warned," I reply. "Love you, Nan."

"Love you too, and Evan?"

"Yeah?"

"I can't wait to meet Imogen and the girl," she reveals.

A smile breaks out across my face, knowing that's her way of letting me know I have her approval. She ends the call, and I look down at the phone, still smiling. Only my nan could make me smile when I'm still feeling angry over Denny and the shit that came out of her mouth.

When my phone rings again, I expect it to be Dad, but it's not. It's William.

"Yeah?"

"You need to come in. Now!" is all he says before ending the call.

My gaze is immediately drawn to Kennedy. *She's here, and she's safe.*

Yet there's a churning in my stomach that has me twisted up inside.

I don't have a good feeling about William's call.

CHAPTER
TEN

KENNEDY

The house is eerily quiet with Evan gone. Imogen went down for a nap not long after her bottle, so I've been left to stew on my thoughts.

I resent my sister for leaving me in this mess. It was cruel to Imogen, and unfair to Evan who has taken it upon himself to try and fix it.

I can't stop my mind from overthinking the entire situation. Evan looked scared when he found out who my attacker was—and he doesn't remind me of a man who scares easily.

I don't know what it means for me, or if I'll live to watch Imogen grow. It scares me so much, and I'm petrified going to the police has made it worse.

Although I don't doubt Evan will protect me, I have to wonder at what cost. I should be grateful I get to stay with Imogen, but then, did I only make things worse by doing that?

My mind can't compartmentalise all these thoughts, not when I'm still reeling over the kiss. And holy-amaze-balls, he's a fantastic kisser. I can still feel the buzz on my lips from where he kissed me. It was only one kiss, but my entire world changed in an instant. I gave him my heart and he never even asked for it.

My feelings have nothing to do with him being good looking or strong. They aren't about gratitude for everything he's done. Or even how attentive he has been towards me.

It's him.

He has taken pieces of my heart, bit by bit, and that kiss cemented everything I had been trying to ignore.

He means something to me, and it has nothing to do with the fact he's Imogen's father.

I'm still in shock over the whole conversation we had earlier out by his car. His words, the meaning behind them, will forever be embedded in my memory. For him to think of me already as her mum is just... It's all I ever wanted, and it overwhelmed me that he didn't take it away from me. I knew I was risking my relationship with her by approaching him, but it was a risk I was willing to take because I wanted her to have everything. She deserves to have her father.

Ever since he made the declaration, I've wanted to scream 'she's mine' from the top of my lungs.

Everything has happened so quickly I've not really had time to absorb it.

My life was boring before Vicky turned up pregnant. I went through life doing what was expected of me. I worked, I paid my taxes, and went home. I kept myself to myself because my life revolved around Vicky and the messes she got herself in. We might not have spoken much, but it didn't stop her from calling when she needed money—that she knew I would never give her—or when she needed a safe space to stay. I've lost count of the amount of times I picked her up from the police station.

Imogen gave me a purpose I didn't know I was looking for. Vicky and I might not have had the best relationship, but she gave me my girl.

Since I'm not good with sitting around, I head into the kitchen to start dinner. He said he would be back for six, so I have it ready for quarter past.

When he doesn't show up by six-forty-five, I start to eat without him, feeling guilty. I don't eat much because I'm too anxious about where he is and what he's doing.

It's half eight when I hear the key in the door. He walks in looking grim and worse for wear. I immediately sit up from the sofa, where I've been lounging for the past hour watching some soaps.

"Is everything okay?" I ask, my pulse racing.

The look he gives me tells me all I need to know. This isn't going to be good news.

"I've got something I need to tell you," he says, sitting down on the sofa next to me.

"Oh, no! What is it? What happened?"

"Drake got let out. He has an alibi that the police checked out, and without any further evidence, they can't keep him."

"Oh my gosh. What is going to happen? I didn't lie to you, Evan. It was him," I remark heatedly. I don't care who else believes me as long as *he* does.

"Hey, babe, I know you're not lying. The police know you're telling the truth too, but Drake, he's conniving. He knows how to manipulate everyone around him. He has always managed to stay one step ahead of the police. I think he knew you would go to the police and had the alibi ready."

"So, what happens now? I wait around for him to do something to me, or worse, to Imogen?" I cry. "Could today get any worse?"

"Um, yeah, it can," he reveals, placing a hand on my shoulder. "That's not all I needed to talk to you about. I may or may not have gone postal on his arse, and he knows you're here, with me."

My head flies up to Evan, and I gasp. He looks apologetic, and I know he's sincere, but I have to get Imogen somewhere safe.

"I need to get Imogen somewhere safe. He can do what he likes to me, but I can't risk Imogen, Evan," I declare frantically.

I stand up ready to go, but he pulls me back down and I land on his lap. "Stop!" he demands.

I ignore him, panting heavily as I think of where I can take Imogen so she is safe. "We have to get her somewhere safe," I repeat.

I squirm in his lap, and I feel him harden beneath me. "Oh gosh," I rasp, biting my lip.

Evan makes a noise at the back of his throat, the sound sending a tingle between my legs. It's been so long since I've been with anyone sexually. Having him this close, this turned on, is doing nothing to keep my mind focused on what really matters.

"I'm not going to let him hurt you *or* Imogen. I think he knows that and will hopefully back off. He should know by now not to fuck with anyone on my team," he brags with conviction.

I turn to his beautiful face. "But what if you can't? I honestly don't care what happens to me. But if anything happened to Imogen, I'd never be able to live with myself."

He presses in closer, his breath fanning across my face. "I don't know what the future holds, Kennedy. But you and Immy, you have already come to mean something to me. You might not care what happens to you, but I do."

I sit on his lap, stunned completely speechless. I've never had anyone talk to me like that, or tell me that they care for me the way he just did.

"We don't know each other," I whisper honestly.

Although sometimes, I feel like I've known him my whole life. The rugged, tattooed, handsome man has brought me to my knees. I shouldn't be so shocked. He caught my attention the second I laid eyes on him.

"We know enough. That's all that matters," he promises, cupping my cheeks.

His lips meet mine, and just like earlier, my entire body sags into his embrace, and I kiss him back. His lips are fuller than mine, and cover them in a hard, deep kiss, his tongue sensually moving in sync with mine.

My body turns when his hands on my hips move me, and now instead of sitting across his lap, I'm straddling him, both legs bent on either side of him. He lies back against the couch, and I follow, my lips never once pulling away from his. He's like a magnet, pulling me towards him.

My hands move up to his strong, broad shoulders, and I can't help but admire the strength and hardness as I do. He's built of stone.

I already knew he was well defined in the muscle area, but to feel it with my own hands causes a flow of wetness to gather between my legs.

"We shouldn't be doing this," I mumble, pulling away.

I keep my gaze on his swollen lips, captivated and wanting more. So I do, leaning in to kiss once more. I can't get enough. I've never felt such satisfaction from just kissing someone—not that I've had a ton of experience. It always bored me before, and my ex-boyfriend didn't help. He smoked, and tasted how I assume an astray would taste. I didn't get any pleasure from it.

Until now.

Until him.

He pulls away, his eyes filled with desire and clouded over with lust as he watches me. "This is a brilliant idea," he softly argues, capturing my lips.

His hands on my hips glide under my T-shirt, and the rough pads of his fingertips run along my ribs, until his thumbs are lightly touching underneath my breasts. My back arches into his touch, wanting him to pull down the cups of my bra to give me the attention I'm begging for.

Imagining him touching me so intimately has me rubbing my sex against his erection. The ache between my thighs becomes too much to bear.

"We have Imogen to think about. If this goes wrong, it could cause a rift between us," I murmur, my lips hovering over his.

He pulls away, and my shoulders drop. I know he's seeing reason, and doing this for Imogen, but it still hurts that it has to be this way. Sadness creeps into my bones, making me shiver.

We've not known each other long enough to take this step either. I get people start somewhere, but I've never been one to jump into things headfirst. I've always weighed out the pros and cons first.

Still, he makes me want to jump in feet first.

"Yes, *we* have Imogen, and like I said to you earlier, I can't predict the future. However, I can promise that no matter what, we'll each be in Imogen's life," he begins, rubbing the tip of his finger over the crease between my eyes. "You're thinking too hard. Just feel what you feel for me, Kennedy. Don't play what if, because I'll just throw some more back at you. What if this was meant to be? What if everything works out for the best? There are always other choices to go along with, Kennedy, but I need you to make your choice and mean it."

"Evan," I whisper.

"Babe, tell me. Because if we're in, we're all in," he states. "I'm hard as a rock and have been since the moment you knocked on my door over a month ago."

I stare at him, taken aback by the pure honesty shining back at me. Never in a million years did I think a man like him would want little old me. But he does. And more, he's willing to make it work.

He's also right. I do have a choice. I could choose to ignore this connection and probably miss out on what could be the best thing to happen to me since Imogen. Or I could see where this goes, and live the rest of my life blissfully happy.

And he's letting me choose.

I nod, agreeing to give this a try, and hope like hell that I don't screw this up. I'm not sure what this is, since he never technically mentioned a relationship, but I want to see where this will go. I want to be with him.

Kissing me deeply, I sigh into his mouth. *I need more.* Thinking we were going to move further than kissing, I'm surprised when Evan pulls away from me with a soft expression. He kisses the tip of my nose, brushing his hand down my hair.

"How are you feeling?" he frets.

"Horny," I blurt, then groan, leaning forward to hide my face in the crook of his neck. "I cannot believe I just said that out loud."

He's still chuckling when he lifts his hand, bumping my chin so I can look at him. "Don't ever be shy to tell me what's going on in your mind. But as much as I love that I'm turning you on," he teases, "I'm on about the whole Drake business."

My cheeks heat. "Oh…" I reply, glancing away. "I'm okay I guess."

"Kennedy," he warns.

I let out a sigh. "Alright, I'm scared. He's going to get away with what he's done, and I'm worried about what he'll do next. I know there's nothing I can do. I can't stop him. I can't fight him. And I most certainly don't have the money to pay him off. Even if I sold everything I own, it wouldn't be enough. All I can do is wait around and see what happens, and that petrifies me," I disclose, taking a breath. "Maybe he will mess up and get arrested for something else. I won't need to worry about retribution then."

"Just promise me you'll stay vigilant."

"I will," I promise.

"You've not been to work the past few days, so I'm guessing you have to go back soon."

"Oh, I have the week off. I thought I mentioned that to you," I point out, thinking back to our conversations.

But come to think of it, I don't believe I did.

"Oh, so I have you to myself for a few more days?"

I smile. "You do."

"Want to do something with Immy? I know she's young, but we'll take pictures so she can see them when she's older," he suggests.

"Sounds awesome," I agree.

He grins, and before I can mention there is dinner in the microwave, he shifts me until my back is to his front and we're facing the television.

"Now, let's watch something before Immy wakes up."

I grab the remote, clicking on the menu to see what's on. When I come across C.S.I., I click on the channel. Evan squeezes me on the hips, leans in, and kisses me on the neck. I snuggle back, enjoying this moment.

It may seem weird to some, but lazing around and watching television like this with Evan could be my new favourite thing to do. His large body encircling my small frame makes me feel tiny and safe.

It makes me feel protected.

CHAPTER
ELEVEN

KENNEDY

Rain pelts against the window, the sound soothing and relaxing as I tuck my feet up on the sofa. It's been trying to storm for the past three days, and early this morning, the skies opened.

I don't want to go to work tomorrow. I like being here, and I love the time I get to spend with Imogen and Evan. But it's all coming to an end.

And we never got to take Imogen to the zoo like we planned. Our tickets were for today, but due to the weather, the park closed. Not that I would take her out in this. I don't want her to catch a cold. The temperature dropped yesterday too, and high winds have blown bins over, leaving rubbish flying around.

Evan left not too long ago to grab some bits we were running short on. I don't like that he had to go out in this, but we were down to our last nappy for Imogen and needed other bits.

A knock pulls me from my thoughts, and my gaze goes to the door. Since the last time I opened the door, I upset his neighbour, I'm not overly keen to answer it again.

However, it must be something important for someone to will-ingly come out in this weather. Placing my tea down on the coffee table, I make my way over and pull open the door.

A small woman with white hair is standing there with a handful of bags. Her rain bonnet is protecting her hair, but the rest of her is soaked through.

"Um, can I help you?" I greet the sweet-looking lady.

"My, aren't you a hot piece," she exclaims, and my lips part.

What on earth is going on? I scan outside for signs of another person with her—and for hidden cameras—but nothing seems out of place.

Maybe it's Drake?

It isn't out of the question. He could use this cute little old lady to lure me out, and it would work. There is no way I would be able to say no to her.

And she doesn't speak like the sweet grandma she appears to be.

My lips twitch, because I never expected it to come out of her mouth. It was such a blunt comment.

"Excuse me?" I ask over the pouring rain.

Imogen starts to cry from her cot, and I bite my lip, torn about what to do. I don't want to shut the door on her in this weather, but then, she could be an assassin in disguise.

"Is that my grandbaby?" she coos, pushing past me. The stacks of bags she's carrying hit me in the stomach, where I'm still hurting from Drake's attack, and I hiss in pain. Still, I take her bags, not wanting to break anything.

"I'm sorry, but who are you?" Then I pause, her words hitting me like a truck.

She's Evan's nan. *Oh my gosh.*

If she didn't hate me before, she will now. She's going to think I'm bad mannered. I mentally slap myself, but in my defence, I do have a lot going on. I never put two and two together.

"Let me just go get—" I start, lowering her bags to the floor.

"I've got this, honey. You take a seat and put your feet up," she offers. "I bet my grandson has had you worn out in the bedroom."

She did not just say that.

Oh gosh, she thinks we're sleeping together.

Oh no, she thinks I'm a hussy as well as bad mannered.

I wanted our first encounter to go differently to how it went with Evan's sister. I wanted to put on my best clothes, cover the bruises on my face, and prepare myself to answer questions.

Now I've got one of his relatives who thinks I took advantage of Evan and am using him, and one who thinks I'm a rude hussy.

I straighten out my clothes, wishing I put more of an effort in when I got dressed this morning. I'm thankful I'm not wearing my leggings with bleach stains on, and that I decided to put on my over-large cream jumper which hangs off one shoulder. I nearly went with one of Evan's tee's.

My hair has been thrown up in a messy bun, since anything more would only hurt the bruises I have. I didn't bother with makeup since I wasn't going anywhere—and I hardly wear it anyway.

Fiddlesticks.

When I hear her talking to Imogen, I pull myself together and quickly take note of the mess in the room. Evan and I were watching some movies and eating junk food before he went out, so all the wrappers are still scattered across the floor.

Quickly picking up the empty wrappers, I shove them in the empty Doritos packet, then grab the empty glasses before taking them to the kitchen. I finish clearing it away in time for the woman to walk back in, Imogen in her arms—who I'm surprised isn't crying.

She's been due a bottle for half an hour, but I didn't want to wake her, so I left it on the side to cool down. I also know Evan loves to be the one to feed her. He told me he feels empty without her, and it gives them time to bond. But he loves doing everything for her. The love he has for her pours out of him, and it's such a beautiful moment. Imogen never got that from Vicky. She didn't get sweet touches, kind words, or a loving glance.

"I just need to warm her bottle up," I explain, moving into the kitchen to flip the kettle on.

"You take your time. I've got her," she promises.

Once it's boiled, I pop the bottle in the jug and go to get Imogen to get her changed, but there's a knock on the door.

I force a smile at Evan's nan.

"Can you watch her bottle for just a second, please?" I ask, lowering my lashes.

"Of course," she agrees, waving me off.

She goes back to talking to Imogen whilst I pull open the door. Lexi greets me, her knuckles white from holding her umbrella steady. This isn't the first time since our first encounter that she's been back. She has come around often for something or another, and I've seen her hanging around outside, like she's waiting for him.

"Hey," I greet, unsure of what else to say.

Normally, Evan is the one who speaks to her when she comes over, and I make myself scarce, hiding away in the kitchen or in the nursery.

"Is Evan here?" she asks, fiddling with the strap on the umbrella.

"No, he just popped out. Is there anything I can do?" I ask.

She lifts her hand to tuck her hair behind her ear, and her coat falls open. She's wearing a short black dress that shows a lot of cleavage.

In this weather.

Jesus, she must be freezing. She'll be lucky if she doesn't catch a cold, or worse, pneumonia.

"No," she rushes out, before forcing a smile. "Can you tell him I need him to come around as soon as he's back, please? It's an emergency."

"Wait," I call when she turns to leave. "You said it was an emergency. Are you sure I can't do anything?"

"You can't," she replies, leaving me feeling a little anxious.

"I'd watch your arse with that one. She's obviously trying to steal your man," Evan's nan warns.

"She's just a friend," I assure her, before letting out a breath. "I'm Kennedy, by the way."

Please tell me your name.

"I'm Evan's nan," she replies, and I groan inwardly.

"I don't want to call you Evan's nan," I admit, ducking my head as I close the door behind me.

"Well, you can either call me Nan or Mary. Both are fine with me."

"Nice to meet you, Mary," I beam, following Mary into the living room.

"I don't want to sound rude, sweetie—you seem like a sweet girl and all—but are you using my Evan?"

"What? No! Why would you think that?" I ask, feeling my throat close up.

Will all his family make assumptions about me just because of my sister?

"Because, honey, you have bruises on your face that tell me you're in trouble. It just seems too much of a coincidence that it happens to be the same time Evan finds out about Imogen."

"Oh… um… no!" I stammer out, before letting out a breath. "Do you want to feed Imogen whilst I explain everything?"

She holds up the bottle I missed. "Sit down then, girl. I might still be in my prime, but my bones never got the memo."

As she takes a seat on the sofa, I take one in the chair, wringing my hands together. "When Imogen was born, I didn't know who Evan was, where he lived or anything. The only thing my sister said about him was that he was a rat and didn't want anything to do with the baby. I had no reason to doubt my sister," I half lie. Everything that came out of my sister's mouth, I took with a pinch of salt.

"And where is she now?"

"My sister wasn't a good person, but I never thought she was capable of the things Evan told me she had done. The day Imogen was born, she left her in my care and walked out of the hospital. She died not long after because of drugs. She was an addict."

"And they didn't contact Evan then?"

"No one had a reason to. I only found out he was the father through snooping through the belongings she died with," I reveal. "I found out his name and looked him up. At that point, Imogen was still in hospital."

Her nose twitches. "Why?"

"She was premature and born an addict because of my sister. Her health was my main priority, but I sent Evan multiple letters and got no response. I did it long after she was free to come home with me. I didn't give up because Imogen deserved to have at least one good parent in her life."

"It seems she already has one," she softly points out.

"Thank you," I reply, cherishing the compliment. "I grew up without my parents, Mary. When they died, it left a hole in my heart. Aside from Imogen, I have no family. And Imogen was the same, and I didn't want that for her. She deserves to have a father, siblings, aunts, and grandmas. Vicky, Evan and I all have choices. We make our own lives. But Imogen doesn't get to do that. And she never asked for this. So the minute I got time off work, I came here. Evan took a DNA test —which I paid for—and now here we are."

"And the bruises?"

I lightly run the tip of my finger along the one on my cheek. "My sister left me more than Imogen. She left me her debts," I reveal, gulping. "The day Evan and I got the results was the day the guy she owes money to turned up. He beat me and threatened Imogen. If I don't pay, he is going to sell her. That is why I am here. Evan knows who the guy is and is helping me. And you should know, this wasn't my choice. I would do anything for that little girl, even if it meant I had to hand her over to Evan—which I was going to do. I pleaded with him to take her because I knew he could protect her, but he brought us both here."

I don't add that I have feelings for him. I don't want to complicate things more.

I really like him. And spending the last few days with him has only intensified that feeling.

"Well, I don't believe that's the only reason you're here," she teases, and just like that, she throws me off guard again.

She went from accusing me of being here with ulterior motives, to hinting at something else.

She's off her trolley.

Thankfully, the key inserting into the door pulls her attention away. Evan steps inside, shaking droplets of water from his hair.

My mouth falls open, and I exhale on a sigh. My gaze zones in on the single droplet dripping from his top lip. I fight the urge to go over to him and kiss him because he looks so flipping hot right now.

He clears his throat, and I meet his gaze. He smirks, ready to say something, but then does a double take of the room.

"Nan, what are you doing here?" he quizzes before shooting me an accusing look. "You knew I wanted to feed Immy." He pouts and it's so darn cute.

"Well, Evan, it's nice to see you, too," Mary quips.

"And who is this?" He gestures behind him.

I lean over to look around him, seeing an older gentleman outside the door, grinning sheepishly at Mary. "He interrogated me for me sitting in the car."

"We're sex buddies," Mary reveals.

I gape at her honesty, whereas Evan groans, covering his face. "Nan, please never mention the men in your life again. Jesus."

I place my hand over my mouth, smothering my laughter. He glowers at me, but I shrug. He did warn me his nan was crazy, but all I can see is a woman living her life. In the best way.

"Well, I only had a onetime fling with a woman, but I was too drunk to remember it. But if you want details on that instead, I can make it up as we go."

"Jesus. Fuck, Nan, tone it down before you scare poor Immy and Kennedy away."

"Alright. Now you can sit and tell me how you're going to help my girl," she demands in all seriousness.

"What on earth are you on about?" he asks, taking his jacket off.

He walks over to where I'm sitting, lifts me up, and takes a seat, pulling me down on his lap. I try to scoot away, but he grips my hips, pinning me there.

Mary gives me that knowing look, and I fight the urge to stick my tongue out.

"Peter, come in, darling, and sit down," Mary orders, tapping the sofa next to her. He wipes his shoes on the mat before following her instructions. It's then I notice there's an age difference between them. Mary is definitely older.

Evan tenses beneath me when Peter places his hand down on Mary's thigh.

"Oi, hands to yourself in this house," Evan barks, causing Mary to giggle.

I just stay quiet, fascinated by the whole thing. This is so weird, and not at all like the families I grew up with. If I had spoken to my nan like that before she died, she would have beaten me with a wooden spoon.

Peter moves his hands with a frown, and places them on his own lap. Mary gives Evan a glare but doesn't argue with him.

"Now, Nan, explain," he demands.

"Well, I was talking to Kennedy here and she explained her situation. Now I want to know how you're going to keep our girl and my grandbaby safe."

My chest expands from her concern. I didn't think my explanation would be enough to get them to understand, but it clearly was. Until now, I didn't even know if she liked me or not. Evan walked in before she could really comment on my situation.

"We're dealing with it," he assures her, before giving me a look.

His eyes crinkle at the corners, and I can feel how happy he is that his nan has taken a liking to me. I didn't realise until now how much it was bothering him.

I never wanted him to fight with his family. He has never felt what it's like to be without them. I do. And it hurts every day. There is no one I can go to.

I wanted Imogen to grow up with tons of people around her so she never felt alone.

Something I never had.

But hopefully with Mary now on board, his sister will come around.

And everything will be okay.

CHAPTER
TWELVE

EVAN

O ut of all the days my nan has to show up, it has to be the day I decide to make a move on Kennedy. I made an excuse to go get some shit from the store, which we did need, but I had ulterior motives. I needed to get condoms.

I wanted to wait, to set the tone and pick the perfect moment, but I couldn't go another day without making her mine. Having her so close, yet so far away, has been keeping me up all night with a hard-on.

Everything she does turns me on. She shakes her hips when she's washing up. She struts when she walks. Her touch, her flowery perfume, and the softness to her voice... It's alluring and erotic.

Even when she tends to Imogen, she gets to me. I picture her being pregnant, reading Imogen a bedtime story.

I've officially gone crazy.

It's the only logical explanation I can come up with for all these thoughts running through my mind. I've found girls attractive, and I've bedded a few, but none of them got me spinning inside. Not like Kennedy.

The desire in her eyes when I walked through the door had me forgetting the man I caught snooping at the house from inside his car. I wanted her. I have from the minute she showed up at my door, stumbling over her words.

Then to top it off, my nan not only chose the wrong day to show up, but she had to go and mention her own sex life—ruining mine completely.

She's always been like this. The woman has no filter. I'd avoid her at all costs, but she's the kindest, most loving and loyal person you could ever know, and I love her. She's always been there for us—especially for Denny—since we were little. She could always see through the fake façade going on at home and knew that they made Denny's life hell. If she hadn't lived so far away, she would have done more for us. But she did what she could when she could. Her big heart knows no bounds.

"So he won't hurt her? Because I'm telling you now, Evan Smith, if she gets hurt again, it will kill me. My heart can't take it anymore. Since Denny's assault, I haven't been the same," Nan retorts, her expression crumbling.

I officially feel like shit. I always expected my nan to outlive us all.

"Nan, I promise, I've got it handled. And have you had your heart checked out?" I ask gently, and Kennedy gives my thigh a squeeze.

"Trust me, your nan has years left in her, son. She has more stamina in her than what any woman did when I was your age," Peter brags, winking at me.

He fucking winked at me.

She's my nan, asshole.

I growl in anger, but Nan laughs it off and puts her hand on fucking Peter's thigh, giving it a squeeze. "Why don't you get the bags, darling. They're by the door," she orders.

He gets up like a good lap dog, grabbing a hundred bags from the hall.

"What the hell?" I gape, seeing baby brand names on most of the bags.

"Why don't you finish feeding Imogen while I show you what I got? She needs winding," Nan remarks, addressing Kennedy.

Kennedy stands up, and I follow, quickly grabbing her by the hips to sit her back down. I kick the pouffe next to the chair she's sitting on before taking Imogen from Nan.

"Hey, princess. Have you enjoyed meeting your nana?" I coo, smiling at her.

She doesn't make a noise, but that doesn't bother me. She's still so tiny, and I know she's behind in her development. I don't care though; I know she'll succeed in the future. With hard work and good parents, she'll do it. I'm sure of it.

"Now, I got this for Kennedy," Nan starts, pulling out some ear plugs.

"Nan!" I remark, offended. "She's not going to ignore Immy when she cries."

"That's not why I got them. They're so she doesn't have to lose sleep listening to you snore," she snaps, looking amused.

I glance at Kennedy, silently pleading with her to defend me and tell my nan I don't snore. But she laughs, keeping her lips sealed.

I glower at her, before aiming it at Nan too. I do not snore. Or at least, I don't think I do. But now she's brought it up, I'm worried I've kept Kennedy up since we've shared a bed for the past two nights. It's been cold in the living room because the radiator is broken, and I wasn't going to turn down her offer.

"And this is for you, grumpy. Hopefully they'll cheer you up," Nan teases, throwing a box at my feet.

I glance down, a whimper slipping through my lips when I see what it is. I try to kick them under the sofa, but it's too late. Kennedy sees them and starts laughing.

"Glad someone finds it funny," I grumble, kicking the box of condoms away from us.

"Peter said to get you some lube. He explained young ones today love all the backdoor business," she states.

I begin to choke, hard enough that Kennedy steps in, taking Imogen from my arms.

"Jesus, Nan. You couldn't have just bought me a watch?" I whine.

She used to bring me a new one every time she visited. I felt grown up with them on, and as I grew out of the cartoon ones, she started to get me expensive ones. I can appreciate a good watch. What I can't do is use a box of condoms my nan bought. I would think about it and kill the mood.

"Sorry. Denny has told me to tone it down, but I just want to be *in* with the in crowd. I don't want to be one of those snotty, knitting, sagging, buggy pushers that need help wiping their own arses," she admits, shrugging. "I'll never be one of those, or the grandmother who sits reading a boring newspaper to find out what's changed."

She's fucking blunt, I'll give her that.

Kennedy laughs, and I glower at her. "She technically got them for the both of us."

Her cheeks turn a faint pink colour. "Evan," she whispers.

I address Nan's concerns next. "Nan, you'll be in a home one day—"

"Young boy, go wash your mouth out. If I go in a home, you grandkids are moving in with me, and your spouses, and your kids, and every fucker else I know. Because the only other way you'll get me into one of those old bag homes is when my body is stone cold and six feet under—and even then, it will be against my will."

"Seriously, just… just stop," I plead, feeling a headache forming.

I listen to her go on about everything she bought, explaining each outfit and toy to us. It's driving me mad, but Kennedy doesn't seem to mind. When she starts going on about getting Imogen christened, I know it's time to say goodbye.

If and when we decided to get Imogen christened, I want it to be mine and Kennedy's decision, not my nan forcing us to.

"It was so lovely to meet you, honey. I promise to get in touch with Denny and explain everything," she whispers to Kennedy, thinking I can't hear. I give her a growl and gently push her further out of the door.

When they're gone, I shut the door behind us and lean back

against it, taking in a deep breath. It feels like I've been holding my breath since the box of condoms came out.

There's a knock on the door, the sound vibrating against my back. My eyes widen as I meet Kennedy's gaze. "Maybe if we pretend we're not here, she'll go away," I whisper, unable to move.

Kennedy laughs and pushes me out of the way to open the door, but soon stops when she sees who is on the other side. Her entire body tenses.

What the fuck?

Peeping around the doorframe, my hands automatically go to Kennedy's waist. Lexi is standing there in the pouring rain. She looks sad, lost, and I can't help but feel sorry for her. I feel like she pushed me away as a friend when she started dating. Ever since Kennedy moved in, though, Lexi has been coming round here more and more. She's either asking me to fix something, put something up, or help move something. When that ran out, she decided to cry on my shoulder about her past, and I couldn't leave her a mess. But I'm starting to resent the fact she keeps pulling me away from my girls.

And it's not like I can ignore her where the house is concerned because I own it and it's my duty to fix it.

Still, I'm disappointed to see her again because I want to spend my time with Imogen and Kennedy. "Oh, hey, Lexi."

"You didn't come," she states sadly.

My brows pinch together when I hear a whispered 'fudge' coming from Kennedy. I still find it hilarious when she replaces swear words with something else. My favourite has to be 'oh my gosh.'

"Sorry, we had visitors. I was just getting around to telling him," Kennedy explains brightly, but it's forced.

"No problem," Lexi replies, and I glance away from Kennedy in time to catch the snotty look Lexi gives her.

Seriously, what the fuck have I missed?

"What did you need?" I ask, keeping my voice pleasant—even if I am fighting the urge to slam the door shut.

We got Immy to sleep ten minutes before Nan and her bloke left, so we've got a couple of hours at the most before she wakes up again. I want to spend that free time with my woman under me, crying out my name.

She fidgets with the sleeve of her jacket. "The, um, the sink is leaking. I can't get it to stop."

I quickly glance down at my watch, noticing it's still before five. They'll be open. "I've got a number for a local plumber. Give him a call and I'll foot the bill," I promise, about to grab the card from my wallet.

"I'm sure it's nothing," she rushes out. "Can you just take five minutes to look at it?"

Her plea has me torn, so I glance at Kennedy. She shrugs, lowering her gaze.

She's no freaking help.

"Okay, but if it needs work, I'll have to call him," I warn. I slide my boots on, grabbing my coat and wallet. Lexi leaves, and I reach down, pressing my lips to Kennedy's. "I won't be long."

"It's fine," she assures me, and I duck into the rain, rushing around to Lexi's.

I'm drenched by the time I get inside. Not wanting to mess around with pleasantries, I walk straight over to the kitchen sink, noticing there isn't a leak.

"Lexi, there's nothing wrong with the sink," I point out, turning around. "What the hell?"

Lexi has stripped down to her knickers and is blocking the only exit. I spin back around, covering my eyes with my hands for good measure.

This is nothing like the Lexi I've come to know. If this had happened a few months ago, I'd probably be hard as a rock right now and jumping at the chance. But that was before. Before I knew what it meant to really want someone.

Now I have Kennedy in my life, and I'd never be foolish enough to jeopardise that. Which is why I'm pissed Lexi is blocking my exit.

Kennedy is my future. She's the one I want. I got lucky the day she showed up in my life with Imogen.

"Lexi, put your clothes on," I demand.

"Don't you still want me?" she coos seductively. "I made a mistake, Evan. I want you."

Her voice sounds closer, and I jump when I feel her fingers touch my back. I push past her, averting my gaze as I move to the door.

Gripping the handle, I reply, "I'm with Kennedy. Her and Imogen are my life now," I tell her. "You don't want this, Lexi. Not really. You made your choice crystal clear."

"Then why can't you look at me? You want me, admit it," she cries, and her words get my back up.

I turn, keeping my gaze on her face and not on her body that she has on show.

How fucking dare she?

I switch to my interrogation mask, wanting her to know I'm dead fucking serious. "Lexi, I'm not looking at you because I respect the woman I have waiting for me next door with my fucking daughter."

"You don't want her though. You want me."

"No, Lexi, I don't. I thought at one point I did, but it wasn't real. I just wanted what my sister had with her bloke," I admit, not feeling the least bit sorry when her expression drops. "I don't know why you've suddenly had a change in heart, and I don't care. You need to stop all this shit now, because I won't put up with it."

"Evan, please," she pleads. "It's you I want. You saved me. You know what I went through."

"I'm not your white fucking knight," I snap. "Have some self-respect, for fuck's sake. I'm telling you the woman next door means something to me and you are still fucking trying."

"If she meant something to you, you would have already left."

"Oh, I'm fucking going," I snap. "Don't ever fucking try this again."

I leave, slamming the door closed behind me. I hear her sobbing, but I keep going. At one time, seeing her cry was my weakness. I wanted to make it right. I always do when I see a woman cry.

But she pushed too far.

Kennedy is curled up on the sofa when I walk back in, and all my troubles go away. She is who I want to be with. Everything about her just feels right, and it was never like this with Lexi. I pushed for those feelings because I was desperate for them, but now I have the real thing. And I never want to let it go.

"Hey, what's wrong?" she worries, sitting up.

I hang my coat up on the hook and brush my fingers through my hair. "Lexi," I answer, wondering how I'm going to tell her.

"I'm taking it she told you she wanted you?" she guesses, taking me by surprise.

I drop down on the sofa beside her. "What? How?"

"Oh, come on; the woman has been pining over you ever since I first arrived. She wants me gone, that much is obvious. So, how did it go?"

"She got naked," I blurt out.

Kennedy shoots up from the couch, and I follow.

Shit.

"Did you… Did you…" She glances away, but I see the tears she's failing to keep at bay.

"Please don't cry. I don't want her; I want you. I promise I didn't even look at her. I got out of there as soon as I could," I assure her, hoping she knows how much she means to me.

She lowers her gaze. "So you didn't… Nothing happened?"

I wrap her in my arms, pulling her flush against my chest. "No. Never! I promise. I'd never do that to you, babe."

She drops her head to my chest. "Fudging hell! We've been giving this a go between us for not even a week and I've already gone all territorial on your bum."

My lips twitch at her honesty, and I lift her chin so she'll look at me. "I think it's brilliant, and hot… and sexy," I whisper, bending down to give her a kiss. She reaches up on her toes, meeting me halfway.

The minute my lips touch hers, I'm lost. Lost in her and lost in the kiss. Damn this woman. She can bring me to my knees with one simple touch.

My hands reach for her jumper, and I slowly pull away when I start to lift it up her body. She's shaking, and I can see goosebumps breaking out all over her skin and chest.

The second her jumper hits the floor, my mouth reaches for hers again in a heated, passionate kiss.

I'm about to grab my own T-shirt, still damp from walking across to Lexi's and back, when Imogen starts crying. I groan into the kiss, hoping she'll stop. She doesn't; she only gets louder. I gently push away from Kennedy, feeling the sexual frustration. I've never wanted to be inside a woman as much as I do her.

"I think our daughter is cock-blocking me," I admit on a groan.

Kennedy laughs, her cheeks flushed and her lips swollen. She reaches down for her jumper, and I try to stop her from putting it back on.

"I'll go settle her down."

She giggles, looking down at my crotch. "Um, I think *you* should settle down first." With that, she walks down the hall towards Imogen's nursery, still laughing.

Little minx.

CHAPTER
THIRTEEN

KENNEDY

Waiting tables was the last thing I wanted to do when I woke up this morning. I wanted to be at home with Imogen and Evan, but my time off—and Evan's—has come to an end.

Spending so much time together over the past week has brought all three of us closer together. I know Imogen is too young to realise anything has changed, but I've noticed she's grown attached to her father.

Just like me.

We've got more in common than I realised. We've bonded over it, and have gotten to know each other on a deeper level because of it.

We've spoken about our pasts, our families, and what we were like growing up. We've shared our likes and dislikes and other random things. Our connection feels stronger, and it feels like we've known each other a lot longer. I even told him at one point that he knows me better than anyone else, and he shared the same sentiment, saying he's never shared this much with his family or friends.

He's everything a girl could wish for in a bloke.

Evan is the first man I've ever lived with intimately, and it's taken a lot to get used to it. I've been self-sufficient since I was a little girl and am used to having my own space.

All of it has been new to me, but it's not all pleasant. There are things I miss about living on my own, and using the toilet is one of them. I got an upset stomach from dinner he ordered in a few nights ago, and I was in so much pain. My stomach curdled, and from the sound and the feel of it, I knew I was going to get diarrhea. And I did. I was completely mortified because it wasn't like a normal poo, where you could shove toilet roll down the loo to smother the sound. It was loud and unforgiving. I know women need to go too, but for me, it didn't feel very ladylike, and I didn't want him to be turned off by me.

I've never been in that position before, but never once did he make me feel uncomfortable about it. Then a few hours later, the same stomach cramps hit Evan, and he made light of it.

There are other things that have been a transition too. Like now when I clean, I'm no longer sneaking around like I'm going to get caught snooping. We've been working on things as we go, but there are somethings we've not been able to.

He never remembers to put the toilet seat down. I've fallen into the toilet in the middle of night because of it. He never puts anything away. His idea of cleaning is shoving it in a cupboard where it can't be seen.

But my biggest pet peeve is spending hours ironing his clothes, only for him to throw them at the bottom of the wardrobe.

The one thing I did think would be a problem for me was sharing a bed, but it's not. I could never sleep in the same bed as my exes. I found it uncomfortable and would barely sleep because I concentrated too much on my breathing.

With Evan, it's not like that, and I enjoy being in his arms. Although, most nights, the sexual tension suffocates me. I want him, and the urge to touch myself whilst in the shower is becoming more and more frequent.

"Order up," Howard shouts from the kitchen, snapping me from my thoughts.

I place the last glass on the shelf and rush over to the hotplate stand. I rip off the table number hanging on the strip above, and groan when I find the food for table four.

Three men walked in over an hour ago, and the air in the room shifted. I'm not usually one to judge, but they gave me some serious creepy vibes. And as the saying goes: if it smells like trouble and looks like trouble, then it most likely is trouble, and these three men were definitely trouble.

They took a while to order, and at first, I thought it was because they were waiting for someone to arrive. But when no one did, and they ordered, it made me wary about going over. It didn't help that the biggest man of the bunch kept staring at me, and each time, a cold shiver raced up my spine.

If they're here to deal drugs to someone, then they'll be extremely disappointed. Mark, the co-owner of Molly's, used to be a policeman. He still takes the term 'serve and protect' seriously, even if he is retired. He won't stand for a mess like that going on in his cafe.

Thankfully, I get off in a couple of hours and won't have to worry about them. I've been dead on my feet since nine this morning. It's now five in the evening, and I have to pick Imogen up from Melanie's soon.

With the weather being so bad, her day care called me this morning, telling me they were closed for the day. Apparently, most of their staff travel from a small village half an hour away, and it's all flooded. They apologised profusely, and explained it was too short notice to get any substitute teachers in to cover for them.

"Can I get you anything else?" I ask as I drop the three plates down, trying not to curse.

I normally only carry two plates at a time. However, I didn't want to hang around them any longer than necessary, so I placed one of the plates along my arm. The hot plate has burnt my pale flesh, leaving an angry red mark.

"Yeah; how about your number?" the biggest suggests, slapping my bum.

I squeal, jumping away. Glaring at him, my pulse races. "If that's all, I'll leave you to your food," I snap, not caring if I get into trouble. I don't deserve to be harassed like this.

Customers are always right, my butt.

"Hey, not so fast. How about you join us?" the smaller of the three asks.

When he winks at me, I shudder. "No, thank you," I remark sternly, before walking off.

On my way back to drop off some extra napkins to a family of five, I hear their crude comments. They can't even keep their voices low, so other tables surrounding them hear too.

"Yo, Kennedy, you got a call," Molly—the main owner—calls, waving the phone in the air.

My lips twitch at the frown he presents me with. He's always complaining about us receiving personal calls at work. Fortunately, since he was here when I got the call about Vicky going into labour, and then again when I was told she was dead, he doesn't mind me taking them.

His frown is probably more due to the fact he thinks I might have to rush out before my shift ends.

The hairs on the nape of my neck stand on end as I take the phone. "Hello?"

"Kennedy?"

"Melanie? Is that you? Is Imogen okay?" I ask, hearing Molly whine under his breath before he leaves to go back in the kitchen.

"Yeah, she's fine. I went over to your place to get her lullaby pen to settle her down a little. But when I went over..." she explains, and I hear her exhale, like she's debating whether to tell me or not.

"What is it? Just tell me," I plead, unable to take the suspense. It's making my stomach ache.

Whatever it is, I can handle it. Nothing could be worse than what happened to me last week and the threat on Imogen's life.

"Your place is completely trashed. I'm sorry, honey."

It isn't the worst news she could have given me. However, a majority of our belongings are there. Evan forced me to only take essentials so that if anyone went back there, it wouldn't look like I left.

I will not cry. Not at work.

I've spent years making it a home. It wasn't much, but it was mine. I dread to think of how much money it will cost to replace and repair everything. I won't be able to afford to replace a fraction of what is in there, not even if I take on extra shifts.

I don't want to start over either. That would feel like a major step back in my life, and I've fought hard to get here. I can't expect Evan to support us forever either. It doesn't feel right, and so far, he's paid for everything I've needed since moving in with him. And when he finds out about this, I know he'll want to fix it... and I can't let him.

"Let me talk to Mo. It's pretty busy today, but I'll try to get over there as soon as possible," I promise.

I don't know if it's from the time off, or if it's from how busy it is, but my feet have never hurt this much before.

"Do you want me to call the police?"

I think it over for a second before answering her. "Let me come and assess the damage, otherwise I'll never get in there if the police are involved. I'll call Evan on the way over and see what he says."

"Okay, sweetie. I'll just see if her pen is usable before I lock up behind me. Be careful on the roads. The weather's getting worse out there."

"I will," I assure her. "See you in a bit." Static greets me. "Melanie?"

Placing the phone back on the holder, I shrug it off. The weather has probably cut it off, or she could have lost battery. Knowing I'll see her soon anyway, I head into the kitchen.

"Mo?" I call, and he looks up from flipping a burger. He gives me a look that says *I know what you want.*

Mo is a large, loveable man, and without him, I would never have been able to raise Imogen on my own, especially without having to depend on government support. He made sure to be fair when it came to my hours and always, always lets me take my own tips home.

The rest of the staff put theirs in a pot, and at the end of each month, it's shared out equally. I tried to refuse, not wanting to be singled out, but because all the other staff members are either old or have no family, they said it was only fair. They even give me a percentage of their tips if my own tips are low at the end of each week.

Pressing my hands together, I give him a sweet smile since he already knows what I want.

"Go. Do whatever you gotta do, but girl, you owe me hours," he warns, holding up a spatula. "God, you're a pain in my arse."

"You love me really," I tease. "Thank you, Mo."

"Get gone," he orders, his lips twitching.

Laughing, I wave goodbye and head to the staffroom to grab my keys and coat from out of my locker.

I'm glad Evan let me bring my car to work. After we dropped off Imogen with Melanie, he had planned to take me to work. I refused because I didn't feel like being stuck if something came up. I wanted to be able to get in the car and leave if there was an emergency. Once he heard me out, he reluctantly agreed. It also helped that his mind was on Imogen, who he struggled to leave. He kept wringing his hands together, and he looked so conflicted. It was cute. It reminded me of me when I first had to leave her.

He even tried to bribe me to call in sick, but I couldn't afford any more time off. I didn't say that to him, though. I never want him to know how hard I struggle financially—although he probably has an idea after seeing my flat. It isn't that I'm poor because I earn a bit of money. But I only earn enough to cover bills and essentials.

I wave goodbye to the others as I leave, and exit out the back where my car is parked.

While running through the rain to my car, I end up getting soaked. The rain is coming down heavier, and I understand Melanie's comment. My flat is only fifteen minutes' drive from here, but with how heavy it's coming down, I'll be lucky to get there in thirty. My car isn't the best to handle in the elements, and the wind isn't exactly on my side tonight either.

Shivering, I start up the car, turning the heater on full blast. Cold air blows through the air vents and I shiver uncontrollably. I really should start saving for a new car. I sit for a few more minutes and wait for the heater to warm up.

When it's warm enough, I reverse out of my spot with ease. The roads are slick as I pull out onto the main road. There aren't many cars around, which eases my worry about driving. I'm not at all surprised that no one is out driving in this. You'd have to be insane. Like me.

I pull my phone out of my pocket and dial Evan's number to update him on what's going on. I know if I tell him after, he'll be pissed. Not entirely at me, but because that's just how he is. The phone continues to ring, and I let it go to voicemail before ending the call. I'll try again later. Without him to distract me, I turn on the radio.

Still, my mind drifts back to my flat. It could be a coincidence that it's been broken into, but it wouldn't be the first in my building. It could be kids after noticing I've not been home. Yet a nagging feeling coils in the pit of my stomach, scared it might be Drake. If he's gone back to find me, he could have noticed I've not been there in a while and smashed the place up out of anger.

Please let it have been kids.

Dialling Evan again, I wait for him to answer, but it rings straight to voicemail. This time, I decide to leave a message, hoping he'll listen to it before I arrive at the flat.

"Hey, Evan, it's me, Kennedy," I start, groaning at how dorky I sound. I fudging hate leaving voicemails. My voice never sounds like me, and I hate it. I sound more like a little girl sucking on helium. "I'm heading over to my place. Melanie called and said there was a break-in and the place is trashed. Call me back when you get this."

As soon as I've ended the call, my phone begins to vibrate in my hand, causing me to jump. I notice Melanie's name is flashing on the screen, and answer.

"Oh, Kennedy! Kennedy," she chokes out, and my heart stops. "I'm so sorry."

"Melanie! Melanie! Calm down," I shout, the signal weakening as I drive through a small tunnel.

"She's gone," she wails down the phone, her voice breaking up.

"Who's gone?" I ask, fear evident in my voice. In my heart, I know who she's going to say, and I can already feel the loss. I close my eyes briefly, not wanting to believe this is happening.

"Imogen," she cries.

Imogen's name echoes down the line, and just like that... my entire world stops.

The voice in my mind screams, and my stomach bottoms out.

No, no, no.

The car swerves, but I quickly straighten the steering wheel with shaky hands, but not before a few cars honk their horns at me.

I end the call without a word, her cries not doing me any favours right now.

She's just a baby. An innocent baby. She can't be gone.

None of this feels real. The tyres splash through the rain, the engine vibrating with the stress of me accelerating, and the radio becomes white noise.

I slam my hands against the steering wheel, screaming out in pain and anger.

"Imogen," I whisper, before a loud, angry sob slips past my lips.

I wipe my tears away furiously. Now isn't the time to get upset. She needs me.

I should never have taken her to Melanie's. I should have known being that close to the flat would be dangerous. I should have stayed at home with her like Evan wanted me to.

This is my fault.

Evan.

He will know what to do. He will get her back. If anyone can help me, it's him.

Reaching for my phone, I redial his number. I've never needed anyone more than I do now in my entire life. I've always done things alone, but with him, I'm not.

I just hope he forgives me for bringing this into her life. For her being gone.

"Goddamn it, Evan," I scream, listening to his voicemail once again. My phone beeps, alerting me of my bad signal, so I quickly rush on. "Evan, it's Imogen; she's gone. Melanie said she's gone—"

My phone slips from my fingers, and I don't get to finish what I needed to say. I hear it clatter near the handbrake, and a whimper slips past my lips.

Scared, desperate, and needing him, I reach for it, not ready to give up.

That's when everything goes from severe to chaotic. My whole life flashes before my very eyes, and I scream out in panic when the car swerves to the left-hand side. I try to take back control of the wheel, but everything happens too fast. My foot slips down on the accelerator, and before I can brace myself for the colossal impact, I clip a car.

The sound of metal crunching, glass smashing, and my own screams fill the car as it spins. Shards of glass cut into my face and arms, and warmth flows down the side of my face.

Suddenly, everything around me comes to a standstill, and the deafening noise of horns blaring and the people's screams stop. The only sound I can hear is the rain hitting the roof of the car. I glance down at the blood dripping in a pool on my lap. I lift my hand up to my head, grimacing at the sting pulsing from a gash there.

Panting heavily, I look around in a daze, wondering what the hell happened. Everything seems to be moving slowly. My gaze moves to the windshield, squinting when bright lights shine through, blinding me.

It takes me a couple of seconds to realise what is going to happen, and my eyes widen.

I brace for impact, covering my head with my arms. I barely have time to reach up before the sickening crunch of metal hits my ears. My whole body is jerked to the right side of the car, my head smashing against the door. Images of Imogen and our life flicker through my mind like a slideshow, just before everything turns black, silencing all the chaos that is going on around me.

CHAPTER
FOURTEEN

EVAN

My balls have shrivelled up from lying on the ground in the pouring rain. Not even the thorn bush we are hidden in gives us shelter from the heavens. This is the part of my job I hate the most, but it's the most effective.

"Can we not call it a day?" I grit out, my teeth clattering together. *Fuck, it's cold.*

"Stop fucking whining. You never whined this much before," Harris grumbles.

"That's because I've never had anything to go home to. Now I do, and I'd rather be there with them," I remark.

I promised Kennedy I would have dinner ready before she got back, but at this rate, I'll be picking up takeout on my way home.

"Well, she needs to get used to it," he states.

"Fuck off."

"Come on, fucker. Show your face," Harris hisses as he slides his body towards the farthest end of the bush. Once he's in position, he pulls the camera from behind his back. I follow suit, grabbing mine.

A dad has hired us to get some evidence against the person who murdered his thirteen-year-old daughter. The official report states she died of a drug overdose, but her dad isn't giving up and wants the person who sold them to her to pay. Most of the information he had was just hearsay, but it did help point us in the right direction. Although we can do things the police can't, it doesn't mean he'll get the results he wants. Our job is to find proof and pass it on. Anything after that is out of reach.

I never had it in me to tell him he was just paying us to do their job. The police don't care about his daughter; they only care about the new drug dealer on the street and want to be the ones to capture him.

Which is why they are on standby, waiting for us to capture the money shot.

"So, when do I get to meet this new piece of ass?" Harris asks, amusement in his tone.

I shoot him a glare. "Never, you fucking wanker. And she's not a piece of ass, you dickhead," I whisper-yell across to him. Gritting my teeth, I warn him. "If you refer to her that way again, you'll be shitting teeth."

He chuckles, not bothered by my outburst. "Oh yeah? So, no chance of tag-teaming?" he teases, and I lose my shit.

I reach for him, but the smirk drops, his features turning serious. "Get ready," he warns.

Peeking through the lens on my camera, I suck in an audible breath. I snap picture after picture, making sure I capture the entire encounter going on in front of me.

The man reminds me of a villain in a Viking movie. His black, curly hair falls down over his leather jacket, framing a face with naturally hardened features. A thick scar bisects his top lip, and his eyes are permanently narrowed into a glower.

He hands a bag of coke to another low-class dealer and rolls out a wad of twenty-pound notes.

"Fuck me," I breathe, when he opens the boot to his car, showing more bricks of cocaine.

"Holy fuck!" Harris curses. Wasting no time, he grabs his phone and calls it in. Just as he puts the phone down, my own phone vibrates in my pocket, reminding me that I have a voicemail that's been left unanswered. It's been half an hour since it came through, but I was too busy to even look at the screen. It killed me not to, because unlike before, I have people depending on me now.

"We got him," I muse, smacking my knuckles against Harris'.

This guy had been lacing the drugs with something, and it was killing people. The dad's daughter picked up the wrong drink at the wrong party, and paid for it with her life.

As much of a pain these jobs can get, moments like this make it worthwhile. It reminds me of why I do what I do, and it keeps me going to take down the next scumbag.

This scumbag, and others like him, thinks the rules don't apply to them. It's my job to give them a reminder.

"Let's go," Harris remarks when the police finally make their arrest.

We slide out of the bush, and I'm grateful to be able to go home to my girls. Speaking of... I pull my phone out, spotting two missed calls from Kennedy and one from an unknown number.

Fuck's sake. First time she calls me, and I don't fucking answer. She could need something, and I've just made myself look unreliable.

Walking to the car, I click on the voicemail Kennedy left me, smiling when I hear her voice.

"Hey, Evan, it's me, Kennedy," she begins, and I smile wider at how awkward she sounds. "I'm heading over to my place. Melanie called and said there was a break-in and the place is trashed. Call me back when you get this."

My smile falls. "Fuck!" I hiss.

She'd better not have gone there. It could be a trap, or worse, it could be a warning. She doesn't need to see the mess her place is in, or see any surprises he may have left.

I should have answered.

Harris nudges me. "What's going on?"

I brush my fingers through my hair. "We need to go. Kennedy's place got broken into and she's heading over there," I tell him quickly.

My gut churns, and I reluctantly press play for the next message.

"Evan, it's Imogen; she's gone. Melanie said she's gone—"

My stomach bottoms out at the sound of her screaming. Horns blare, glass smashes, and I can hear rubber spinning on tarmac.

Harris hears and is the first to move, rushing over to the car.

"Kennedy! Fuck!" I yell, knowing she can't hear me.

The voicemail cuts off, leaving me with nothing. I don't know if she's okay. By the time I reach the passenger side, Harris has the engine going.

The second the door closes behind me, he has his foot on the pedal. I fly back in my seat, my heart racing.

"Where am I going?" he asks, briefly sparing me a glance.

And that's it. I don't know where the fuck to go. Kennedy has been in an accident, and Imogen has been taken. I want to tear myself in two so I can be there for both.

But I can't. Not until I get all the information. "We need to go to the hospital," I tell him, trying to remain calm.

I'm glad I programmed Melanie's number into my phone this morning as I hit call on her number. I wanted to make sure she had a way of contacting either me or Kennedy if anything happened. Really, I just wanted to check in on Imogen throughout the day—something I never got to do.

I'm just hoping Kennedy's mistaken, and Immy isn't gone, but in my gut, I know it's true. I can feel it. It's the same feeling I've had since I woke up this morning. I thought it was about the job I knew we would be on today. If I knew my girls would be at risk, I wouldn't have let any of us leave the house. William told me he had someone keeping an eye on Drake.

"Oh my god, Evan. Kennedy hasn't arrived yet, and I'm beginning to worry. She should be here. The police keep asking me all these questions, and I don't know anything," Melanie cries, her voice hoarse. "I'm so sorry. So fucking sorry I couldn't protect her."

"Miss, we need you to answer some more questions," someone in the background asks stiffly.

Prick.

There's no sympathy, only annoyance. A child has been taken, and it's clear Melanie is hysterical and needs calming down. Making her answer the same questions over and over will just cause her anxiety to increase.

"No, you don't. I need to answer the father's questions. He needs to get his little girl back," she snaps, sniffling. I find myself respecting her in that moment, but hearing her say 'father' and 'his little girl' causes my chest to tighten.

I'm trying my hardest to keep my cool, I really am, but fuck, she's my little girl. I've just got her. I can't lose her.

No one will know how to calm her down. They won't know to take her blanket. She hadn't been in the best of moods before we left, and I'm worried they won't have the same calm and patience with her like me and her mum do.

My anger spikes, fearing the unknown.

"Melanie, I need you to calm down for me. What happened?"

"I went over to Kennedy's to get Imogen's music pen, hoping it would settle her down. When I got there, Kennedy's place was a complete mess. I quickly called her, and she told me she was on her way. I was going to see if the pen was still in working order. I swear; I turned my back for a minute. Someone hit me around the head, and when I woke up, Imogen was gone. I'm so sorry. This is all my fault."

My heart sinks, and my hands clench into tight fists. I want to kill someone. I know who did this, but I need to have some sort of proof. I begin punching the fuck out of the dashboard, unable to hold in my anger any longer. The pain in my fist does nothing to release the aggression inside of me; it only fuels it more.

"Evan! Fuck! Calm the fuck down," Harris demands, his arm smacking me in the chest and holding me back. I breathe heavily, my chest heaving. Melanie says something down the phone that I don't quite hear, but it's enough to bring me back to the present.

"Okay. Okay," I reply, combing my fingers through my wet hair. My training kicks in, and I get it together. "Did you see anyone unusual? Someone you've not seen before who seemed curious about you or Kennedy's place?"

"I... No... Oh, wait. There was a guy yesterday knocking on her door for a good twenty minutes. He had a scar on his face. I also noticed him this morning outside, just before you guys turned up. I didn't think anything of it. God, this is all my fault. That poor little baby. What have I done?" she wails, and my heart breaks, knowing all too well who she is on about.

"This isn't your fault, Melanie. You're lucky he only hit you around the head. He could have killed you," I tell her honestly, thinking back to his rap sheet.

He's brutal, and should have been put away years ago. We've never been able to get any charges to stick though.

When I went to the police station, he was smug. He knew we couldn't charge him because of his tight alibi and lack of evidence.

"You know him? You can get her back? Where is Kennedy?" she asks, somewhat calmer.

"I think she's been in an accident," I admit, pinching the bridge of my nose. I'm torn about what to do: find my girl or go to my woman. As soon as I've checked to make sure she was indeed in an accident and is okay, I'll go home and find everything I can about this son of a bitch. He's going to wish he never messed with Kennedy or Imogen when I'm through with him.

"Oh my god. Where? I'll be there—"

"Miss, you can't leave," a policeman remarks.

"Melanie, I have to go. We're just pulling up at the hospital. Stay where you are and I'll call you when I find anything out," I promise.

"Okay, okay," she rushes out, and I end the call.

Unable to wait for Harris to park, I jump out of the car with it still moving. Harris honks his horn and shouts obscenities out of the window, but I ignore him, sliding over the bonnet and rushing through the emergency doors.

"Hi, I'm Detective Smith. My fiancée, Kennedy, I think she was in an accident around half an hour ago. Can you tell me if she's here?" I ask the receptionist frantically.

She forces a smile, and I want to snap at her to hurry when she doesn't answer quick enough. "What's her name, sir?"

"Kennedy. Kennedy Wright."

She types quickly into the computer, but then a man with a white lab coat walks around the desk, watching me. And I know in my gut it's bad. He heard me say Kennedy's name. He knows who I'm talking about.

"Are you a relation to Miss Wright?" he asks, putting his hand up to the receptionist to stop her search.

"Yes, I'm her fiancé." I lie easily, and I do it because I know it won't be long until she does have a ring around her finger and is taking my last name. Both of my girls will.

"Your fiancée was brought in not long ago with severe head trauma and multiple injuries," he explains, and I follow him as he takes me down a long corridor.

Out of nowhere, Harris is standing next to me. I'm grateful for his presence. There's only so much I can take before I explode again.

"Is she okay?" I ask when the doctor stops short suddenly.

"It's too early to tell. She has a broken leg, fractured ribs, and a lot of cuts and bruises on top of her head injury. Her broken leg won't be put in a cast until the swelling reduces. We've managed to clean up all her scrapes, and wrap up her ribs. At this time, we're concentrating on her head injury. We're waiting for the CT scan to open up so we can send her down. Once we have the results, we'll be able to tell you more about her diagnosis."

I groan into my hands, suddenly feeling sick. She needs to be okay. She has to be. She has Imogen to look after. I need her. Imogen needs her.

Fuck! *Imogen.*

The doctor opens the door to a private room, and gestures me inside. I wish he'd prepared me more for what I was about to see, because as soon as I see her small, fragile frame lying down on the bed —broken and bruised—I collapse to the floor on my knees. I've seen crimes that would make people sick to their stomach. I've been called out to scenes that have been horrific, but nothing could have prepared me to see someone I've come to love, lying helplessly in bed. We don't even know if she'll be okay.

I've never seen her look so vulnerable as I have in this moment. I thought I did when I showed up after her attack, but this… God, I'm looking at a shell.

Her head is swollen, and cuts and bruises already have her face swelling. She's barely recognisable. The pounding in my chest tightens, and I feel like I'm suffocating.

"Is she in pain?" I whisper, my heart hurting for her.

"We've made her comfortable," the doctor answers from the end of Kennedy's bed.

Not caring who sees me, I sob into my hands, feeling defeated. I let this happen. I should have been there for her. I should have let her drive my piece of shit car knowing I only needed it to get to our offices. I should have done a lot differently this morning, but my biggest regret is not telling Kennedy that I love her. In only a week, I've given the woman my heart and my soul. I'd die for her.

Why the fuck is this happening? She's a good person. She deserves a long, full, happy life. She doesn't deserve the life she's been given, not at all. It's unfair.

Standing up, I walk to the edge of the bed, my anger simmering to boiling point when I see her close up. Taking her delicate hand in mine, I silently promise her to make all of this right. Pulling away, my hands clench into fists and my jaw locks.

"Mate, you need to keep it together for a little while longer," Harris warns, snapping me out of my thoughts.

Wiping the tears from my cheeks, I look up at him, knowing he's right. There's no point in me standing around feeling angry, and waiting for the doctors to tell me something when I have my little girl to find. And I know when Kennedy wakes up to find Imogen still missing, with me at her bedside, she will hate me forever. I can't have that.

"Doc, I need you to do me a favour. I know you're busy, but our daughter has been kidnapped. It's how Kennedy got into an accident. She was trying to get back to the woman watching her," I reveal. "I need to go find our little girl, but I don't like leaving her alone. Can you call me on this number if there are any changes, please?" I hand him my card. "Any at all; I don't care how insignificant it is."

He pats me on the shoulder, his expression grave. "I'm sorry about your daughter. I hope you find her," he replies. "I have a few other patients I need to see, but I will make sure to keep you updated. I'll pass your number on to her nurse too."

Knowing that's more than I could ask for, I nod. "Thank you," I rasp.

Walking back over to Kennedy, my heart beats frantically at her pale face. I bend down, my lips to her ear, before whispering, "I'll find her, I promise. Just make sure you fight and be awake when we get back. I love you, Kennedy."

I lift my head, giving her a soft kiss on the lips before leaving. Harris falls in step beside me without question. He hasn't asked any questions at all. He's blindly followed me around, just looking out for me, and waiting for my word.

I'm guessing he's caught on to what's going on, though.

"What's the plan?" he asks when we reach the car.

I open the door before meeting his gaze over the hood. "No plan. I find him and I make him pay. Simple."

Harris doesn't look too pleased with my reply. I've always gone into a job knowing everything. But those jobs, I never had something to lose.

Now I do.

He'll pay for hurting my woman.

He'll pay for taking our daughter.

And I'm not going to stop until he does.

CHAPTER
FIFTEEN

EVAN

It seems finding Drake is harder than I first thought. I hit all his known associates first, and came up with nothing. All of them pretended to not know who I was talking about. My knuckles are swollen and red from beating answers out of them. But they either feared him more than they did me, or they truly didn't know where he was.

They're small fish in a big pond, so I didn't really expect them to know anything. I just had to get my frustration out some way.

And the self-employed contractor William put on Drake has taken the day off. Today of all days. I left William to deal with him, but so far, he has no clues as to where Drake might have taken her.

And none of his reports give any indication to Drake planning this.

We're no closer to finding Imogen, and I'm starting to think I failed her. Her mum gave her a shit start to life, but I wanted to give her the best future. And in a split second, it was taken from us. She's not even old enough to understand and know we are coming for her. She is probably crying her eyes out, wondering why we aren't there for her.

The doctors have called a few times, saying things still aren't good with Kennedy. I want to be there as much as I want to be here, but I meant what I said back in that hospital. I can't go back there until I have our daughter. She would never forgive me, and if I'm honest, I would never forgive myself.

I promised to protect them, and I've done a shit job of it so far.

Since we got no answers from his associates, it left us no choice but to head back to the bungalow and go through everything I have. The door has been left open, and Harris has stayed outside, barking orders to anyone and everyone he thinks may be able to help us.

My mind is so focused on getting my girl back and getting back to the hospital to my woman, that I don't care about the mess I'm making.

Papers are scattered all over the floor in the front room, and I'm grateful I never gave in to Kennedy's plea to get rid of them. It bothered her that they were here, but I had to keep them close in case we needed them.

And we do.

Fuck do we need them.

I understood her anxiety. I had my own concerns. If she read half the shit in these files, she would feel sick to her stomach like I do.

I hardened myself to a lot, but this guy... he takes no prisoners.

I've kept them out of sight so she didn't snoop. I never wanted the light in her eyes to fade, and over time, it would have. She's pure and innocent, and these files contain ugly and true evil.

I also didn't want her to come across the pictures. They aren't as easy to look past, and some of them involve her sister. They include his victims, and the people who betrayed him or stole from him. I knew if she saw them, she would run to protect Imogen.

"Fuck's sake," I shout, growing more and more frustrated.

Time is ticking away, and the longer it takes me to find him—to find Imogen—the less likely it will be I'll find her. I have no idea what he plans to do, but I can't imagine any of it is good.

"Hey, Evan. Do you have a minute?" Lexi greets, her voice soft.

I stiffen, not wanting to deal with her. "Fuck off, Lexi. I don't have time for your shit," I snap, throwing a file against the wall near to where she's standing. "Fuck!"

"What's wrong?" she asks, not giving up.

I glower at her. "I don't have time to talk to you, Lexi. Seriously, leave."

"No, I won't," she argues. "You were there for me when I needed you, and you clearly need someone right now. Tell me what is going on?"

"My woman is in the hospital, and my girl has been kidnapped by some fucking psychopath. Are you happy now? Because as you can see, I don't have fucking time for your shit."

She flinches at my raised voice, her entire body tightening like I just struck her. I've never yelled at a woman like I just did to her, but I can't find it in myself to care right now. I might have done if she hadn't of done what she did, or if my mind wasn't on my girls.

But she did, and it can't be erased.

I'll also never forgive her for forcing me to spend what might have been my only time with my girls, fixing pointless crap.

They aren't dead.

Fuck's sake. I scrub a hand down my face, exhaling heavily. Kennedy's all alone in that hospital with no family sitting by her side to show their support.

My daughter is God knows where, and I dread to think of what situation she's in.

She sniffles. "That's not why I'm here. I promise."

I brush my fingers through my hair. "I don't care."

"Oh, Evan. What's happened? Who's with Kennedy?" she asks, only concern lacing her voice.

"No one," I whisper, and slump down on the floor, the reality of it all hitting me.

There is nothing in these files that tells me anything I don't already know.

Drake moved in with his dad and step-mum when he turned fourteen because his mother was a junkie. They are the only living relatives he has, according to his file. And since I've already searched all his associates' homes and businesses, there is nothing else left. He has no romantic relationship or regular hook up. Or he hasn't since we had someone watching him. William's guy reported back with a pretty detailed statement of Drake's whereabouts, and all those stones have been turned upside down.

"I'll go to the hospital and sit with her. I'll tell them I'm her sister," Lexi assures me, but I ignore her when I hear her start talking to Harris.

Something in this file has to help me find where the fuck he took my daughter. He has to have another place he goes, somewhere he doesn't visit on a regular basis, or hasn't been on the police radar.

Harris tells Lexi that it's a good idea, but I have no idea what they're talking about. But then a name stands out in a file. The biological mother. And it hits me. We've been hitting up his dad and step-mum's house, when all along we should have been looking into his mother and her background.

From what it says, she had no visitation rights to Drake, but when he turned eighteen, he found her and they formed a relationship. Speculation in the file says she's the reason he got into selling drugs to begin with. His mum's poison is heroin, which is what the police think Drake sells, amongst other shit. He's known for other crimes too—anything to make money.

"Fuck!" I yell out, getting up off the floor.

Aaron walks in at that moment, glancing around at the papers thrown across the room.

"You got anything?" he asks, watching me with downcast brows.

I know I'm losing it.

I know I don't look sane right now.

But I don't need his pity.

I need his help.

"Yeah. Were all these up-to-date when you had them copied and sent over?" I ask, pointing towards the mess.

"Yeah, why?"

"I think I know where he's taken Imogen. Harris, are you coming with me?" I call out, before jerking back to Aaron, wondering who told him to come here. Last we heard, he was getting the picture of Drake sent out to the local police stations. "How come you're here? Not that I mind; I could use all the help I can get."

"I'm picking up Lexi to take her to the hospital," he tells me, looking to his right, to where Lexi has thrown a bag of stuff together. *Why the fuck is she packing Kennedy's stuff?* My anger rises again, but then I notice she's packed some of Imogen's belongings too, and I stop still. She must have sensed my stare because she stops what she's doing and turns to me.

"You're going to find her. You're going to get her back, and when you do, she will need the comfort of her own things. I've got some things for Kennedy too. I know I've been a shitty friend and I've made things awkward between us. I came over to say I'm sorry. But then this happened, and I... I just want to be here for you all."

This is the woman I came to know and care for.

I force a smile, grateful she thought of all of this. Kennedy has no one, just like Lexi. All her family either disowned her or passed away. Her ex wasn't the best of people, and her family weren't the brightest either.

But unlike Lexi, Kennedy has me now. She will always have me. I'm not going anywhere.

"Thank you," I choke out. "Please call me once you know how she is."

I walk over, kissing her temple, before grabbing my keys off the side.

"I will. I promise. Just bring your daughter home. And be safe. They need you."

"I'll drive," Harris calls out, and I hear his keys in his hand.

I stop, turning around, not having time for this shit. "Mine has Imogen's car seat," I yell back.

"You're also blocked in," he snaps, and that's when I notice a car has pulled right up to my car, leaving me no room to pull out.

"Fuck," I growl, kicking the tyre of the offender's car.

Fucking prick needs parking lessons.

CHAPTER
SIXTEEN

EVAN

The drive over to Drake's mother's house feels like it's taking for-fucking-ever—and it isn't just the weather slowing us down.

Every light we come across turns red. Every crossing has had kids or other people crossing. It's like the world is out to stop us from getting to where we need to go.

Finally, we pull up to the country road leading to the mother's house. I'm literally bouncing in my seat, ready to take this fucker down.

Taking a sharp bend, the car skids to the side. Harris straightens the vehicle, but it's too late. The car ends up on the side of the road. He tries to reverse out, but the tyres skid, mud splattering up the side of the car. Putting the car into gear, he tries to move forward, but the car does the same, spinning in the mud.

We're fucking stuck.

I slam my hands on the dashboard, growling. "This is just fucking great."

The backend wheels are spinning like crazy, mud flying all up the side of the car. Harris and I exchange a look, before I jump out into the pouring rain, running around the back of the car.

"One, two, three," Harris shouts, revving the car. Mud splatters out from under the tyres and sprays all over me. So not only am I soaking wet, but now I'm covered in fucking mud.

I push hard, my strength coming from all the pent-up anger I've been harbouring for the past couple of hours. I'm close. So fucking close to getting Imogen back, and this happens.

My heart sputters to life when the car jerks forward, the movement nearly causing me to fly forward. I catch my footing before my face meets the ground, and rush over, jumping back into the passenger seat.

My foot taps nervously on the car floor, and I'm about ready to jump out when we pull up on her street. The tension in the car is suffocating, and I know Harris is feeding off mine. I don't care. I just want my girl back.

"Slow down. If she's in there, you don't want to go barging in and putting her in more danger. Let's take a look around the back. Back-up is on the way. They're five minutes out," Harris warns.

I know all the rules, all the guidelines, and have my own way of doing shit, but tonight? It's just gone to shit. The sky has completely darkened, the moon is covered from the black clouds as the rain still falls heavily. It matches my mood perfectly.

There are cars lining the driveway when we pull up a few houses down. There are more cars on the street, but there's no telling if they're for the mother's house. When I take a look at the house from the file, the lights are shining brightly in every window.

"Well, they're definitely in," I mutter.

"What do you want to do?" Harris asks, scanning the rough neighbourhood.

My phone beeps with a message, and I hold my hand up, silently telling him to give me a minute. I read the message before tapping out a quick reply. "Andrews is here. He's going to watch the front. We don't want to chance that he'll escape."

"So, we go around the back. C'mon."

We jump out of the car and walk up to the neighbour's driveway. I'm hoping the fucker is too wasted to be keeping a look out. I don't want him noticing us until it's too late. I don't want him to see me coming.

We quietly make our way down the side of the neighbour's house, keeping our heads down. The garden is fenced off, so we jump over into what can only be described as a dump.

The garden has been filled with scrapped household items and rubbish. There's a rusty fridge-freezer, a sofa, oven, and even a shopping trolley.

"The woman needs a trip to the tip," Harris mutters in disgust, wiping off a soggy piece of bread that has clung to his jeans.

"I think this is the tip," I reply, before moving slowly towards the backdoor.

We get closer, both of us crouched down under the kitchen window. Slowly sliding myself up the wall, I go to peek through, but a baby's cry has me pausing in my tracks.

"Fuck," Harris whispers.

"Shut that fucking kid up," a woman yells over music and other voices, and my spine stiffens.

"You shut her the fuck up. If I touch the thing, I'm ripping its lungs out," a man roars, earning laughter from whoever else is in the house. I don't stop to think. I'm up, leg raised and booting in the backdoor.

The first thing I see when I barge into the kitchen is that the room is filled with smoke. There are a few guys standing around, but one look at my expression, and they're backing out of the kitchen door.

I don't spare them another glance. I'm too focused on the man standing on the other side of the table.

Drake.

Blood rushes through my veins, and everything happens quickly.

Too quickly.

He moves, sliding across the table, ready to charge, but so am I. We grab at each other in full force, and crash to our sides into the table. The wood splinters around us, but I don't let it stop me.

I move, straddling his chest as I swing my fist back, smacking him across his cheekbone.

"Where's my fucking daughter?" I roar, raising my fist once more.

He grins maliciously, blood coating his teeth. It does nothing to satisfy my need for retribution. I don't think death would squelch this anger storming inside of me.

Punch after punch, I raise my fist, wanting to kill the fucker. All I see is red. I don't care about my job, about going to prison, or anything. I just want him to pay for what he's done.

To my woman.

To my daughter.

To our family.

"You're gonna fucking die," Drake threatens, kicking me away from him.

I fly backwards, and before I have the chance to recover, he's on me. I block his blows like I'm trained, but it doesn't stop him from getting in a few punches.

More noise from the house reaches me, but I can't lose focus. The only person I can see now is *him,* the only person in my mind is *him;* and I'm not going to stop until he's begging for mercy.

Kicking his legs out from under him gives me an advantage. I roll until he's beneath me, gripping him hard around the neck.

"I'm not the one dying tonight," I grit out, clenching my fingers into his flesh.

His face begins to turn red, and I find satisfaction in that for a moment. Until he swings his legs out, wrapping them around my waist until I loosen my hold. The palm of his hand swings up, catching me in my jugular. I wheeze, gasping for breath until he throws me off. I land against the cupboard with a thud, and pain shoots up my side.

More shouting fills the kitchen, along with the sound of glass smashing and other noises. I try to listen out for Imogen, but Drake takes that split second of distraction to punch me in the ear, sending me off balance.

Reaching up, I hit the palm of my hand as hard as I can into his nose. Blood spurts out all over the place, and he howls in pain before kicking out at me again, connecting with my shins. His cries echo in my ears as I get to my feet, trying to steady myself.

Fucking sissy.

I'm suddenly jumped from behind, my legs carrying me backwards from the sudden weight. Whoever the fuck is on me delivers a few punches to my head before I ram their back against the sink, his screams of agony howling across the kitchen. I throw him over my shoulder, thrusting him at Drake, who has just jumped to his feet. It knocks them both to the floor. My breathing is erratic, sweat beading on my forehead and body.

When Drake kicks the bloke away, I'm ready for him. I manage to deliver a few kicks to the ribs, before the wind is knocked out of me. In his hand, Drake holds the thick, broken leg to the table, aiming at my side. My reflexes are becoming slow, and he manages to knock me down to the floor.

There's a loud crash inside the house, and more voices fill it. His startled eyes jump to me before flicking to the backdoor. I can see the decision in his eyes, and before he can make a run for it, I kick my feet out again, knocking him to the floor.

Using all my strength, I roll back before flipping forward to my feet. Once I'm vertical and standing on my feet steadily, I move to the left, circling Drake. He doesn't disappoint. As soon as the pads of his feet are touching the kitchen floor, he tries to move past me for the backdoor. He doesn't get far before I'm swinging my arm out, catching him in the chest. He grunts at the contact, and I give him a smirk.

"Playing with fire, pig," he grits out.

With a force I didn't think he had left in him, he has me by the shoulders and is hauling me across the kitchen, my body smacking hard into the kitchen sink. Cutlery crashes around me, plates and mugs smashing on the floor.

Twisting to the side, I roll off the kitchen sink and straighten up. Grunting, I rush forward, swinging my fists into the side of his stomach. He hisses out in pain at the same time he lands another blow to my jaw, knocking me back a few steps. I soon gain my composure and push him against the work bench on the other side of the kitchen, my hands gripping his neck in another tight squeeze. Only this time, I show him no mercy.

Seeing his rugged scar across his face is just another reminder of how scared Kennedy was of him. Images of her bruised face and body flicker through my mind, and it just causes my anger to rise.

"You'll fucking pay for what you've done to my woman and daughter," I growl. The metallic taste of blood invades my mouth, and it's worse than the smell of blood filling the air in the tiny little kitchen.

"Fuck… you," he chokes out, trying to spit at me.

I laugh, throwing my head back, and I know I sound manic. I'm crazy. I must be. I hear Harris shout something to me, but the ringing in my ears hasn't stopped. It's blurred all of my senses. I can't hear or speak, and I lose all control and reason.

When I look back down into the eyes of the soulless man who did this to my life—my world—I finally snap out of it.

He needs to pay.

Ending his life will be too easy for him. He needs to suffer for the rest of his days. I also don't want to ruin my life by ending his. He isn't worth it, and my girls need me. Going to jail because of a fucking loser like him isn't going to help me get Imogen back to her mother. It isn't going to get me back to them.

I throw Drake off me, pushing his limp body back into the counter with a loud thud. Turning around, I'm about to question Harris when I see something silver reflect in the kitchen light. It blinds me momentarily, enough time for me to notice Drake raise his hand.

Even exhausted, emotionally drained, and only charged by my anger, I move quickly. My hand dashes out, grabbing his wrist in a tight grip. I move forward, shoving him backwards, before taking his hand and slamming it against the cupboard. It takes me a few attempts before the knife drops to the floor. Once it's safe, I move back, and before he can take another swing at me, I rear my fist back, taking one last shot, knocking him out cold.

He falls to the floor in a heap, and I don't bother moving to check if he's still breathing. I just turn to get my daughter.

Harris is there, his foot on a lady's back whilst he holds a screaming Imogen in his arms. She looks filthy. The fuckers haven't even bothered changing her. She's been lying in a shitty, wet nappy. The stench is nearly making me gag. It's soaked through her clothes, the stains visible, and my heart clenches.

She's still screaming her lungs out, her complexion bright red, bordering on purple. Thankfully, I didn't see any other injuries like cuts and bruises. Sadly, I know that doesn't mean she isn't hurt. I've worked with children before and I know not all bruises show.

I keep my eyes locked with Harris' whilst grabbing Imogen from him. The second I get her in my arms, I hold her close, shoving my face into her neck. She cries harder, the sound breaking my heart.

I check her over visually, seeing no signs of any injuries, which causes me to relax a little. But the smell of weed on her clothes has my body tightening all over again.

I need to know if the ambulance is on the way, but when I open my mouth to ask, a scuffle on the floor has me looking down. Harris has still got his foot pressed firmly down on who I presume is the mother.

I raise a brow, wondering what the fuck I missed.

"She resisted arrest," he explains, avoiding my gaze.

He's not telling me something.

"What did she do?" I bite out, wishing I could scrap my no hitting women policy just for a second. The woman is wearing dirty, grubby clothes that are far too big for her. I can see bone sticking out everywhere I look, and when my eyes reach hers, they look just as cold and ragged as her expression.

"Look, the ambulance should be outside in a sec," he assures me, just as I hear the sirens moving closer. I move to the door just as he speaks, his tone rushed, hesitant. "Don't lose your head now. They're going to tell you eventually or you'll hear me inform the paramedic, but she had her hands wrapped around Immy's neck, so make sure the paramedics look her over properly."

I narrow my gaze at the woman on the floor, ready to rip her throat out, but Imogen screams get louder. "Fuck."

I've never wanted to hurt a woman in my life, but I want to kill her.

I rock Imogen from side to side, knowing she comes first. Drake's mum will pay for what she did, just like her son.

Walking out the door, two officers come running up the front garden. "They're in the kitchen. One's knocked out, and one is being restrained," I inform them, and walk straight to the ambulance.

I'm about to step into the back, when a male paramedic stops me.

"Sorry, sir, but you'll have to wait. We have a patient that is unconscious who we need to deal with first," he explains, and I see red.

"No, you don't," I bite out. "You have a five-month-old baby who was kidnapped and strangled to see first. She's filthy and covered in shit and piss. Now get in the front seat and drive us to the fucking hospital."

Although he looks apologetic, he lets his pride get the best of him. He's clearly not the type who gets put in his place often.

He grunts an apology. "I'm going to call for another ambulance, but I'll go check on him whilst my colleague checks over the baby."

I nearly grab him back and tell him the fucker deserves to rot, but the female paramedic holds out her arms for Imogen. I hesitate for a second before handing her over. She's still squirming, her lungs protesting at her hoarse cries.

When I found out about Imogen, I knew I'd worry every second of every day. I'd be that dad. I'd be the one who was over protective, who wouldn't let her date or go out past curfew.

But I also knew I'd be the dad who went to every school play, every sports day and every event she was included in.

But never once did I think I would have to go through this. Never once did it register I might lose her.

That burning pain in my chest hasn't subsided because today, I nearly did.

Today, I failed her.

I didn't protect her.

Now she's hurt, screaming in agony, and there is nothing I can do.

I failed her in the worst possible way.

"Can you tell us if she has any medical conditions?" the female paramedic asks gently, lying Immy down on the bed.

My mind is blank. I know nothing. I know nothing about her medical conditions other than what Kennedy has told me about her birth. She hasn't said anything about any long-lasting conditions.

I scrub my hands down my face before answering her, giving her everything I know. "She was born an addict. I know she had some problems after being born, but I don't think it's ongoing. I've only been in her life for a short while. I'm still learning everything."

The minute the words leave my mouth, I regret them. They might not let me stay with her, and the thought petrifies me.

"Are you the girl's father?"

"Yes," I reply, watching her carefully for judgement, but when I see none, I relax somewhat. It's obvious I'm involved in the law, and the fact I've just announced Immy was born an addict, I can only imagine what they are thinking.

I reach out to Imogen, and straight away, she wraps her hand around my finger. I smile down at her, my heart splitting wide open.

"Can I change her?" the woman asks, and I nod, feeling tears fill my eyes.

I could have lost her. I could have lost her and her mother in the same day. I still don't know what's going on with Kennedy at the hospital. No one has gotten in touch with me since I left, and I don't know whether that's good or bad. Just thinking about Kennedy all alone, hurting and suffering in that hospital, has my heart beating faster and causes worry to form in the pit of my stomach.

I watch as the paramedic gently undresses her, using wet wipes to clean up her body. When she starts sticking pads to her chest, I make a choking sound, my throat closing up.

"I need you to hold her arm for me," she orders.

"What? Why?" I ask, panicked.

"I need to get your daughter on an IV. She needs fluids," she explains as she messes around with her equipment.

Taking a huge breath, I grab Immy's tiny arm in my hand, feeling sick to my stomach as she screams through the needle piercing her skin. The paramedic works quickly and fluently. When she's done, she turns to the front of the ambulance.

I turn in the same direction, noticing for the first time that the other paramedic has returned.

"We're good to go," she calls out, grabbing a few other things off the side.

"Is she going to be okay?" I ask her once the ambulance starts moving.

"I'm going to leave her unclothed for the time being and wrap her up warm in a blanket. Hopefully, now that she's out of her soiled clothes and is getting some fluids inside her, she will be able to settle. She has some bruising on the side of her neck, finger marks clearly the cause. The doctors at the hospital will look over those when we arrive. Her heartrate is a little high at the moment, but it's most likely due to the stress her body is under. Once we have her settled and relaxed, we will be able to tell you more. There are no other clear signs of injury, but we have the best doctors waiting on standby in the ER."

"Thank you," I rasp, watching her tend to Imogen with care.

We're nearing the hospital when Imogen finally falls asleep from exhaustion, her tiny hand still gripping my finger with all its might.

The closer we get, the harder I pray that when I walk into that hospital, Kennedy is awake and ready to greet us. We need her. Imogen needs her.

One way or another, I'm not leaving this hospital without both of my girls in my arms. In fact, once we're home, there is no way I'm ever letting them leave me again.

CHAPTER
SEVENTEEN

KENNEDY

Holy panthers, my head hurts. What is going on? What is that noise? I open my eyes with a struggle. They feel heavy, like they're somehow glued together. I begin to panic, wondering why I don't have control over my body.

I lift my hand, but that too feels heavy. Wetness slips down my cheeks and makes it easier for me to open my eyes. When I do, I'm taken aback when I find I'm lying in a hospital bed. Tubes are sticking out from my hands and arms, and panic grows within me.

My head becomes too heavy to move anymore, and I look up at the dull cream ceiling, wondering why I'm here. What did I do? Loads of scenarios run through my head, but none are making any sense to me. My imagination is running wild with awful explanations, but the headache pounding in my head is stopping anything real from forming.

That's when the pain begins to register. At first, it's just the pounding in my head, like someone has a hammer on the inside and is trying to smash their way out. But soon, my leg, chest—hell my whole body—is throbbing with excruciating pain.

Lifting my hand to my head, I feel a cloth wrapped around it. Panic seizes me, and I need to get up. I twist and turn in the bed, cries of pain leaving my mouth.

Even though my body is about to give up, I'm not. I need answers. Just when I'm about to open my mouth to scream, the door opens and a girl I recognise walks through. She must hear the sound that escapes my mouth, because her head snaps up and she gasps. She's looking at me with a mix of horror and concern.

I open my mouth to plead for answers, but in a blinding assault, everything comes flooding back painfully.

Imogen.

Mel called me. There was a break-in. Then Imogen was taken. Does anyone know? Has Mel called the police? Do they have her? Oh no! What if she's still out there and nobody knows? A strangled cry leaves my mouth.

I throw the covers off me, ignoring the pain that assaults my bruised, aching body. Any other time, I'd feel ashamed, embarrassed, knowing *she* is seeing me at my most vulnerable. It's not a feeling I'm accustomed to. Especially with someone who dislikes me.

Sitting up feels like a chore, a painful, miserable chore. The gown they've dressed me in has an open back, and I feel a breeze hitting my bare skin, causing me to shiver. Nothing is going to stop me from getting to my daughter. Even if I have to wander these halls or the streets dressed in only this.

"Hey, Kennedy, it's me. Do you remember me? It's Denny, Evan's sister," Denny announces, tears pooling in her eyes.

Why is she crying? Has something happened to Imogen? Does she know something?

"You need... You need to help me. Imogen... I need to find Imogen," I cry. The pain in my throat feeling so raw, it's beyond any sore throat I've suffered with in the past.

"Please, calm down, Kennedy. You've been in a serious accident."

"You don't understand," I plead, as she tries to help me lay back down.

"I do. I know about Imogen," she admits, meeting my gaze. "Evan is going to get your daughter back. I promise. But you need to rest and get better."

Her voice is stern, filled with promise and conviction.

"Why are you here?" I ask, my shoulders dropping against the pillow.

I feel so helpless, so vulnerable, and my daughter needs me. I could ignore Denny, but there's a stubbornness in her eyes that her brother also carries, and I know there is no way I can leave. I don't even have the strength to fight her or with her. Not when I need to save my strength for Imogen. She will need me.

"Lexi, Evan's next-door neighbour, called me. She's outside. She didn't think you'd want her in here, but she hasn't left. She wanted to make sure you weren't alone," she admits. "She's worried about you."

Lexi?

Outside?

And Denny is here.

What the fudge have I woken up to? None of this feels real. Not Denny, not Lexi, and not being in hospital.

"Is this real or am I dreaming?" I ask her seriously. She laughs just as the door opens.

"Are there any signs of her wak—Oh, hey, I'll wait outside," Lexi murmurs quietly, her face flushed.

"Lexi?" I call out, stopping her. I want to know why she's here and if she knows anything about Imogen or Evan.

"Hey," she greets, slowly walking over to the bed.

She looks tired and worried, and it surprises me considering what she pulled with Evan. But I know if anyone has answers, she will.

"Where's Evan?" I ask, tears in my voice.

She forces a smile. "He's gone to get your girl," she assures me.

"He found her?" I ask, my pulse racing.

"I'm not sure. When I left, he was adamant she was at Drake's mother's house," she explains honestly.

I gasp. My worry in the car about Drake had been right. That break-in was a set up, a trap to get my girl. But how did he know she'd be at Mel's? It's not like Mel and I go out and party together. All I know is, if she's with that monster, she isn't safe.

His words repeat over and over in my head, the promise he made to sell Imogen, and my vision becomes blurry.

I try to get up again, knowing what Drake plans to do to her. He said he'd sell her. He only cares about getting his lousy three grand back. Three grand he willingly gave a drug addict in the first place. He doesn't care about what my baby will be going through. He won't lose sleep over destroying two innocent people's lives.

"Hey, he'll find her. He loves you, Kennedy. He loves you both. He won't stop until he finds her," Lexi swears, sincerity in her tone.

She doesn't look sad by it, only sure of it.

"He's going to sell her," I rush out on a sob, and the pain in my body becomes too much.

Denny helps me lie back down, but my body remains stiff, and my tears flow down my face.

"Who, Evan?" Denny asks, glancing between us.

I reach for her hand, hoping she'll help me. Evan told me what happened to her, so she has to understand. "No. My sister was into some bad stuff. The man she owed money to came over to my house and beat me. He threatened to take Imogen and sell her. Please, help me get out of here. I need to get to her."

"Oh, God," Denny breathes, covering her mouth. "He will find her. But don't give him more to worry about. He knows you are here and you are safe. If he comes back and finds you gone, it will take his focus off getting Imogen back."

"He knows I'm here?"

"He does. He came here first," Denny explains. "The doctor told us he rushed out, promising to bring your daughter back to you."

"Okay. Okay," I whisper.

"You've been going through so much," she begins, squeezing my hand. "I didn't know, and I'm sorry I never gave you the chance to explain. I'm so sorry for the way I acted. I was being stubborn and stupid. I never meant any of the things I said. None of it was even really about you. My stupid jealousy took over. I just miss my brother."

"It's fine. I understood where you were coming from. I just didn't want you to fight with each other because of me," I tell her, glancing away. "He loves you. He didn't mean to hurt you."

"I know. I just wish I dealt with everything that day a lot differently. Being a mum has changed me in so many ways, but I guess, deep down, I've still got that childishness in me. I've got a lot to learn," she admits sadly.

"You were being an overprotective sister," I point out, and my attempt to smile turns into my lip trembling. "I'm sorry too, for springing all that stuff on you without warning."

"You've got nothing to be sorry for," she assures me.

Lexi clears her throat. "Since we're all on the apology train, I want to say sorry too, Kennedy. What I did was uncalled for, but mostly, I'm sorry because I was in the wrong. I saw him happy and I suppose it got to me because I couldn't find *my* happy. Deep down, I knew I'd never find it with him, but when I noticed he had it, I believed I could have that with him too. It was wrong of me. I'm just sorry I hurt you. You've done nothing but be kind to me, whereas if I was you, I would have slammed the door in my face by now."

I remember all the times she passed judgement when I opened the door. The look she would get in her eyes. Not once did I think she was jealous of the situation. I only saw her jealous of my relationship with Evan.

Knowing she got naked in front of Evan still angers me somewhat. But seeing Lexi now has me realising I've not really met the real her. She looks sincerely worried for my wellbeing and seems like a genuinely kind person. Maybe if I hadn't come along, she and Evan might have worked something out. The thought causes a sharp pain in my heart. Thinking of him with another woman makes me feel sick. But the thought he'd be better off without me has crossed my mind more than once since Lexi walked into the room.

"Please, don't. I can't handle any more. Sometimes I think

everyone would have been better off without me turning up," I cry, feeling sorry for myself.

Imogen's life is ruined, and Evan's will be destroyed if he doesn't get her back. And mine? Mine was doomed the second I got that call telling me she was missing. The only reason Evan is even interested in me is because of Imogen. Without her, there is no doubt he'd be with someone else right now. He would never look twice at a lowlife like me.

My feelings for Evan have grown over the week, and with each day they have only grown stronger. Deep down, I know if it wasn't for Imogen, we wouldn't be together.

Denny must see the doubt written on my face, because she tightens her hand around mine.

"No. Don't do that. I thought Mason was only with me because of Hope, but I was wrong. So fucking wrong," she sighs, smiling wistfully. "He loved me for me; Hope was just an added bonus. Evan loves you. He's never brought a girl home to meet us before… Ever. Not even at school. Don't let your head take you there, Kennedy. I might not know you, but from what Nan has said, you're the best thing since sliced bread."

I nod, absorbing her words. "Thank you," I croak out, before turning to Lexi. "And thank you. For coming here, and staying." A thought occurs to me. "How do you know each other?"

"Lexi called me. I stayed at Evan's for a while last year and Lexi cleaned the house up before I arrived. She still had my number in her contacts. My nan is on her way too. She got stuck on some bridge. The river has overflowed or something, so she was waiting for everyone to turn back around before she could. She called twenty minutes ago telling me she was on her way."

"I don't deserve any of you," I reveal, just as the door opens again.

A man I don't know walks in, followed by another, who I know is Mason. No one could forget that face. He's still as handsome as when I first saw him. I remember Evan telling me he has four brothers, but looking to the man standing in front of him, I know he isn't one of them.

His sandy blonde hair is messy and unkempt. He's larger than Mason but only by so much. He carries himself with importance, a confidence you don't see in many people. He also has a lethal energy surrounding him. Something tells me I wouldn't want to get on the wrong side of him. From the look on Lexi's face when he walks closer, I'd say she wouldn't care what side she got on. I have to stifle a giggle. I mean, how inappropriate would it be if I burst out laughing right now. My daughter is gone, Evan is gone, and I have no idea what the sugar is going on.

"Hey, I'm Aaron. I'm Evan's old partner," the man in front introduces himself.

I nod, biting my lip. It must be the drugs they've got me on because I can't help the next thing that slips from my mouth.

"I didn't know he was gay." When I realise I've said it out loud, I begin to giggle. I giggle so hard that it begins to hurt my sides. My giggles turn into laughter, high, hysterical laughter.

One minute I'm laughing so hard that everything around me disappears, then I'm sobbing. The first one that breaks is painful, and it echoes around the now silent hospital room.

Denny takes me in her arms, letting me sob into her chest.

"I need her back," I wail, my emotions all over the place. I try to get myself together. Being in this state is not going to help anyone.

"I meant work partner," Aaron mutters, and Lexi giggles.

"Where is he?" I ask, sniffling. I don't move, keeping myself locked in Denny's arms, needing her comfort.

Mason walks around the bed, looking between us, and when he looks back up to Denny, his eyes go soft.

That's so sweet, I think when he reaches her, leaning over to kiss her forehead. If only I had Evan here. Even better, Imogen. My heart is breaking having neither here with me. I need them. I'll always need them.

"He's downstairs getting Imogen checked over," Aaron declares, and at first, I think I heard him wrong.

I sit up, wincing when the pain becomes too much. My head and leg hurt the most. Every move has shots of sharp electricity shooting down my body.

"I'm sorry, but could you repeat that—slowly," I order, and this time, focus on his mouth, not wanting to miss anything.

His lips twitch as he rubs the back of his neck. "He's downstairs getting Imogen checked over."

"Oh my gosh. Is she okay? Where was she? Is she hurt? Is she going to be okay? Tell me," I demand hysterically, causing a nurse to rush in.

"What's going on in here?" she asks sternly, eyeing the men in the room warily.

"We're all good," Aaron tells her, holding his hands up before turning to me. "She's fine. She just needs to wait for the doctor to give her the okay to leave before he can come up. I offered to watch over her but he nearly knocked me out."

The nurse walks over and starts checking the machines out. I think I'm in shock because there's nothing I can say. She's been found. She's safe. She's okay. Evan is safe. My heart beats rapidly and the machine next to me starts beeping like mad. The nurse walks over and says something, but my mind is on one thing.

My daughter.

My daughter is safe.

"Miss, I need you to calm down."

"She's safe. She's safe," I wail when it really hits me, and I turn, hugging Denny. I sob into her shoulder just as the door opens again.

Expecting it to be another nurse or maybe a doctor, I pull back. But when a large form looms in the doorway, my breath is taken away.

"Evan," I breathe out, and everything I was feeling seconds ago about us, starts to simmer away.

Because there is nothing but love in his eyes as he meets my gaze.

It consumes me.

Wraps me up and soothes me.

And I know what we have is real.

CHAPTER
EIGHTEEN

EVAN

The doctors finally give Imogen the all clear, but it does nothing to ease my concern.

"Just keep a close eye on her. If anything changes, don't hesitate to call the number on the leaflet I gave you," the doctor tells me.

"Are you sure she's okay?" I ask again.

If there's a chance she's not going to be okay then why aren't they making her stay in for observation?

"Yes. Her blood pressure is back to normal, and she's hydrated. There is no swelling inside her throat but the swelling around her bruises will take a few days to go down. You can take your daughter home, Mr Smith."

I nod, holding a sleeping Imogen in my arms. After being here for a few hours, I'm finally able to check on my woman. No one has been able to give me any new information. All they've said is, she's stable but still unconscious.

Like that makes me feel any better.

Aaron came down not long ago to keep me updated. He offered to watch over Imogen while she was sleeping, but the look in my eyes must have told him that wasn't going to happen. I feel like I've had to choose between the woman I love, and the girl I love, and I've hated every second of it. I even asked at one point if they could treat Imogen upstairs where her mum was, but they told me no.

Arseholes.

We're walking down the corridor, when I hear footsteps rushing toward us from behind.

"Oh good Lord, there you are. My little girl," my nan cries, and I look around, wondering where the fuck she came from. The hallway was clear when we rounded the corner. She must have been running fast to catch up to us that quickly.

"Hey, Nan," I greet, feeling drained. I'm worried sick about Kennedy, and I'm still not sure I should have let them discharge Imogen. I don't care how sincere the doctor looked when she spoke to me.

We're on the floor Kennedy is on now, which is a different ward than the one she was on earlier. When I stop walking to greet my nan, she holds her hands up for Imogen, but I just hold her tighter to my chest. She's still wrapped up in a blanket, though she now has a nappy on thanks to one of the nurses.

I remember Lexi packing clothes for both of the girls. I just hope it was something warm because I don't want my girl being cold. She's suffered enough today as it is.

"Oh, come on, Evan. I've been stuck in bloody traffic feeling sick with worry about my two girls. Let me hold her."

"I'm sorry, Nan, and I mean no harm when I say this, but I'm not letting her go. The next time she's out of my arms will only be to place her rightfully in her mother's," I explain, and her lashes lower before she bursts into tears.

"You're such a good boy, Evan. Come on. Let's go see how my daughter-in-law is doing." She beams. "Have you heard anything yet?"

Her daughter-in-law comment gains my attention. "What?" I murmur, astonished.

How the hell does she know I plan on asking Kennedy to marry me? Not that I'm giving Kennedy much of a choice. After today, I know I won't be able to live without her or Imogen. There's no way I'm letting them go.

"Oh, calm your horses, my boy. I saw the way you looked at her when I came to meet them. But back then, you didn't have wedding bells shining in your eyes. Now you do."

I shrug, not bothering to deny it. I will be marrying her, even if she tries to refuse. I'll drag her skinny, fine arse down that aisle kicking and screaming if I have to.

We reach the door to Kennedy's room, and I instantly hear voices coming from inside before a loud sob echoes through the hall. Her cries hit my chest with a sharp pain, and I have to compose myself before pushing the door open.

Kennedy is crying into my sister's chest when I enter. I can't believe she's here, consoling my girl of all people. Mason is next to Denny, looking uncomfortable. I would laugh if it wasn't for the fact my girl is now looking at me like she has seen a ghost.

"Evan," she breathes.

And the tension I had been holding onto evaporates.

She's okay.

She is awake.

And we can put all of this mess behind us.

"Hey, babe," I greet, and Lexi and Aaron move out of the way.

Kennedy bursts into tears, her eyes locked on mine and her hands reaching for Imogen.

"You've got fractured ribs, baby. Be careful," I warn, and my sister moves out of the way, but doesn't move far. I look up and give her a thankful smile. I'm guessing Aaron called her.

"Lexi called me," she whispers, reading my mind. She looks back down to Kennedy, who is now holding a sleeping Imogen in her arms while sobbing. Denny's expression softens, and her eyes water as she looks down at Kennedy in understanding. She's looking at her in a way only another parent would. There was a time she was close to losing Hope. It might not have been in the same way as today, but I can imagine the feeling we've been suffering with all day was just the same to her.

Looking back at Kennedy, checking her over to see if she's okay, I can tell it's hurting her to hold Imogen. But I also know there is no way she can let her go. She'd walk through fire for our girl.

I turn my head to Lexi and mouth 'thank you' before stroking my girl's face, the part that isn't messed up with cuts and bruises.

"How are you feeling?" I rasp out, overjoyed to see my girls back together.

"So much better now that you're both here where you belong," she tells me, giving me a watery smile. I lean down, kissing the top of her head. "Is she okay? What happened?"

"She's fine. They've checked her over and given her the all clear."

"She's bruised," she chokes out, tears still rolling down her face as she lightly strokes Imogen's hand where the IV was put in.

"Yeah, baby. The paramedics had to link her up to an IV," I start, but pause, not knowing how to tell her about the bruises on Imogen's neck. Kennedy's hand reaches out to squeeze mine, and I give her a small smile.

"What happened?"

"She was taken by Drake. We found her at his mum's house. They've both been arrested and won't get off on the charges. There are too many against them."

"Is that why you're covered in bruises and have a fat lip?" she asks, not taking her eyes from Imogen.

"Yeah," I confirm, and she reaches for the blanket covering Imogen. Before I can stop her, she pulls it apart, noticing the bruises on her neck.

She gasps, lightly running her finger over the marks. "What happened? Oh my gosh, why have they let her out? Is she okay? Are you sure you should be up here?"

"Yeah, she's a fighter. I made sure to get another doctor to double check her injuries. I think towards the end, they wanted to sedate *me*," I tease, trying to ease the mood.

Everyone listens intently, but I ignore them, my main focus entirely on my two girls.

"Why is she naked?" she asks, her nose scrunching up.

"She was dirty from not having her nappy changed, baby. Let's not worry about it now. She's safe and back with us, where she belongs. They can't hurt us anymore, okay?"

She nods, but I know it's only to pacify me. She's still mulling it over in her mind. I lean in, giving her another kiss, when the nurse speaks up. I hadn't even noticed her in the room.

"I'm sorry, but visiting hours are over. I know about your situation so I spoke to the ward nurse and she said it was fine to have two people stay. But I'm afraid I'll have to ask the rest of you to go," she tells us, her lips tipping down.

Aaron, Lexi, Mason and Denny agree to leave and begin to gather up their things. Needing to have a word with my family for a second, I look down to Kennedy before speaking. "Let me go talk to them outside, and then I'll be back." I turn to Nan, who has made no effort to move. "Nan, can you stay here for a second and watch over them?"

"Of course," she agrees, moving to Kennedy's side.

Denny leans over, whispering something to Kennedy before hugging her gently. Mason moves in next, and the poor kid doesn't even know how to address her. He ends up just patting her shoulder a few times before leaning in and kissing her cheek. I'm not going to lie, sister's boyfriend or not, I want to smack his face away from hers.

Denny must have noticed my expression, because she starts to giggle. Taking Mason's hand, she walks out of the room, leaving everyone else to say their goodbyes. I follow behind them, hearing Lexi saying goodbye along with Aaron, before they, too, follow us out.

When we're all outside, I turn to Lexi first. Her eyes widen when she feels my attention on her. Before she can open her mouth, I move forward quickly, pulling her against me for a tight hug. I know she's not expecting it when I feel her body tighten, but I need her to know how thankful I am. How happy I am that she put everything going on aside, and was a friend to me. The friend that I've missed the past few months. Without her help today, Kennedy would be lying in that room on her own, scared out of her mind with worry. For that, I'll be forever thankful.

"I'm so fucking thankful to you, Lexi. For everything," I whisper hoarsely. "It killed me to know she was on her own. You knew that and came. Even after everything."

"Don't worry about it," she tells me, playing it off. I give her another squeeze, before pulling away. She looks up at me with a sad smile. "I hope everything is going to be okay with you all. I'm only next door if you need anything, ever. I'm so sorry for the way I've been acting. I haven't been myself and I'm so embarrassed about it."

"Let's not worry about any of that anymore. Fresh start?" I offer, giving her a genuine smile.

"Yes. I'd like that. Oh, and the bags of stuff I brought with me for Imogen and Kennedy are in the cabinets beside the bed. The nurse said to leave them there. If I had known you were in the hospital sooner, I would have brought them to you and Imogen."

I nod. "Thank you. For everything."

"Call me if you need anything," she repeats.

"Promise."

Aaron steps forward next, patting me on the shoulder. "You need more time at the gym, mate. He really did a number on you," he teases, but I notice the way his eyes darken.

"You haven't seen the other fucker," I retort.

"Let's hope you did a good number on him," he remarks.

He walks off, and his words play around in my head. Drake really did do a number on me. In more ways than one. But one thing he didn't get to do is break me. All I have to do now is make sure he didn't break my woman.

And if he did, I will spend the rest of my life putting her back together again.

I watch as Aaron takes Lexi's arm before walking down the corridor. Seeing them together is another reminder that I need to set the two up. If they haven't already hooked up, that is. Why it never occurred to me to do it before, I don't know.

Turning to my sister, guilt and shame hit me. I said some awful things to her that at the time felt justified. But now, seeing her tear-streaked face, I'm not so sure.

"I'm sorry," I tell her, at the same time she says, "I'm really sorry."

We both force a laugh, but unable to bear it another second, I pull her into my arms, holding her tightly. I've missed her so fucking much. Even before all of this.

I thought I had to distance myself from her to protect her. I did it because of Vivian and her cruel actions. But all I did was build a wall between the two of us.

I should never have left her there when it became too much. I shouldn't have stayed away when I was working on Carl's case. I should have done a lot of things.

"Thank you for coming," I tell her through the dryness in my throat. It must have taken her a lot to come here with how she feels about Kennedy. "I know how you feel about Kennedy, but you still came."

"She's family," she reveals, surprising me. "I was being selfish and childish. I should never have reacted the way I did. You know it was uncharacteristic of me. I've told Kennedy I'm sorry, and I am. But I'm also sorry to you. The way I behaved…"

"It's fine. It's over now. I'm just fucking glad you're here," I choke out before grabbing her into another hug. "And I'm sorry too. I should never have said those things."

"Take care of them."

I kiss her cheek and pull back. "I will, forever."

"We're staying in a hotel not far from here. The bridge is all flooded and the roads are still bad. I don't want to risk us getting into a crash," she explains, and I start to feel bad that she has to spend the night away from Hope. I know it must be hard for her. It would kill me to spend a night away from Imogen now that I've got her in my life. I can now understand why my sister fought so fiercely to keep Hope. I'd do the exact same thing for Imogen.

"Go get some rest. I'll speak to you tomorrow," I promise, wanting to get back to Kennedy.

She squeezes my hand and leaves. I watch her walk down the corridor in Mason's arms. It's then I realise how lucky I am to have the sister I do. She could be annoying like other sisters that I know about through mates, but she's not. She's anything but. She's always been understanding and older than her years. She has clawed her way through some tough times, and I truly admire her for it.

When they're no longer in sight, I turn back to the door that holds my future.

Walking back in, I find Nan has found the bag of clothes Lexi packed and is currently in the middle of singing to Imogen whilst changing her at the end of Kennedy's bed. Neither of them notice my entrance, so I take the time to survey everything. How my life became this in such a short amount of time is crazy, but one thing is for certain: I wouldn't change any of it for the world.

The door opens behind me, snapping me out of my thoughts. Nan and Kennedy startle at the sound, and at seeing me already standing there. I smile sheepishly before moving out of the nurse's way. She walks in carrying a bottle and pushing a crib.

"I pinched this from the maternity ward. Imogen is fine to stay here with you and your fiancé."

I glance at Kennedy, worried about how she'll react. She goes to deny it, but I step in and rudely interrupt. "Thank you. That's really kind and understanding of you. We appreciate it, don't we, babe?"

Her lips part, but there's no mistaking the spark in her eyes at hearing herself be called my fiancée. It makes me really fucking pleased to see she's not disgusted by it.

Taking a seat in the chair next to the bed, I pull it as close towards Kennedy as it will go, taking her hand in mine. When Nan walks around the bed and hands me Imogen, I smile. She's fully awake now, and her big blue eyes are staring up at me.

"I've got to go check into a hotel. The radio has been giving out flood warnings all day so I don't think I'll drive back tonight. I'm going to book in then get some food. Would you two like me to bring something in for you?" she offers, before continuing. "The hospital food isn't that great. My friend Doris had her gallbladder out not long ago here, and said the food was enough to put someone in the hospital."

"Please," I answer, grateful she thought about it.

I grab the bottle the nurse left on Kennedy's lap and start feeding Imogen. Now washed and dressed in clean clothes, she seems happier. She gulps her bottle down like she hasn't been fed, but then I grit my teeth when I realise she hasn't. The only source of food she's had is whatever she had at Mel's, and the IV she got in the ambulance. She could have starved to death.

Fuck! We really could have lost her today. The thought guts me.

The door shuts behind the nurse, and I look up to Kennedy, wondering if she's gone to sleep. She's been really quiet since I walked back into the room, and I wonder if she blames me for everything, but instead, I find her watching me with a look I can't decipher.

"Why do they think I'm your fiancée?" she asks quietly. A pink blush rises on her cheeks and she looks away for a split second before her eyes reach mine again.

"Because you are, baby. You don't have a choice in the matter. It would be hugely appreciated if you would agree though, because as soon as you're well enough, we're getting married."

"We are?" she breathes, and her eyes start to water.

"Yeah, baby. We are," I tell her, softer this time.

I want her to belong to me in every way possible.

"But... But we've not known each other that long," she points out, trying to protest. Her words hold no heat behind them so I know she wants this as much as I do.

"Baby, I knew the day I met you I was going to marry you. It just took me until today to realise that."

"I love you," she rasps.

"I love you too, baby. Now get some rest. We've got forever."

I never thought I could love someone this quickly or deeply.

Today I was scared I lost her. I was scared of a lot of things.

But never once was I afraid to love her.

And I will love her even in the next life.
I will love her for eternity.
I will love her with everything inside of me.
Forever.

SNEEK PEEK

KENNEDY

(**H**)ere's a sneak peek of what's to come in Max's novel, book four in the Carter Brother Series, but in Kennedy's POV)

What the fudge is that God awful sound? My ears are ringing—or it could be a phone—I'm not sure.

What I do know is, I'm never drinking again. Ever! And I mean never. I hate alcohol, and as of today, I'm never drinking the stuff again. Alcohol and I are not friends. We will never socialise furthermore. Ever.

Last night is a complete blur. Little parts come to mind, but nothing that explains why I feel like I'm dying. I feel like I've been hit by a truck all over again.

"Babe, you're going to wake Immy up with your groaning," my husband teases through laughter.

I bury my head further into the pillow.

Evan kept to his word, and as soon as I was better, he hauled me to a registry office where we got married. I've still got my cast on in my wedding photos, but I don't care. The only thing that mattered to me that day was marrying Evan. We also got his name on Imogen's birth certificate, and managed to get her last name changed.

Everything is perfect.

I've never been in love with someone as much as I am with him.

But right now, I want to kick him out of bed. I'm actually kind of missing my cast, because I could use it right about now to kick him out.

"Stop talking," I grumble, pouting into the pillow.

"Babe," he muses, and his laughter causes the bed to shake.

The motion causes a wave of nausea to assault my stomach, and I growl.

After everything was sorted between me and Denny, and Evan and Denny, she became a new fixture in my life. She's declared me her sister, but the way I'm feeling this morning, she's no sister of mine.

It was Denny's hen party last night, hence the reason for my major hangover. Evan skipped going to the stag night because he didn't want anyone else watching Imogen.

Even though neither of us blame Melanie for Imogen being taken, we've both agreed to watch over her ourselves. It's only until the memory of what happened to her isn't so fresh in our minds, and we're comfortable leaving her with someone else.

Melanie feels remorse for what happened, but agrees she couldn't handle watching over her again. What happened scared her more than we realised. She's getting better now, but still, after eight weeks, I had hoped she'd visit us more or let us visit her.

The ringing starts back up, and I grunt into the pillow, wishing the noise would stop.

"Babe, it's Denny. She's called a thousand times already this morning."

Moving my head, I wince at the light in the room and narrow my eyes on Evan as he hands me the phone. He chuckles, kissing my forehead.

"I'll get you a coffee," he whispers before moving off the bed. I watch distractedly as he walks away, his tight buns tensing in his boxers.

Fudging hell, my husband is hot.

"We're not friends anymore," I grumble into the phone, feeling the room spinning around me still.

Denny screams, and I pull the phone away from my ear, wincing at the ear-splitting sound. "Calm down and stop the shouting," I yell, but flinch at the pain shooting in my skull.

"I need your help, or someone's help. I think I cheated on Mason," she cries.

At first, my mind is shocked that she'd cheat on him, but then I vaguely remember her being carried off somewhere by Mason himself.

"No, you haven't. He brought you home, didn't he?"

"I don't know. He's not here. I'm walking over to Joan's now. I can't believe I've cheated on him. I'd never do this. I can't even remember last night. What the hell happened? Why did I wake up wearing half of a hooker's outfit, and how the hell did I get a fucking tattoo?" she demands hysterically.

I moan down the phone, not remembering a thing. Every time an image pops into my mind, it's blurry. I don't know what's real and what's not.

"You got a tattoo?" I croak, my voice dry and hoarse.

"Yes, it's actually really awesome, but that's not the point. I don't remember getting the fucking thing. Please, what did we do last night?"

"I honestly don't know, Denny. I remember dares," I tell her, and I can't help but giggle at her hooker statement. "You've really got on a hooker outfit?"

"Kennedy, it's not funny," she cries. "I'm wearing leather. Fucking leather. I'm a mother, for Christ's sake. What the hell did we do? Hold on, I've got a message."

I hear her pressing buttons on her phone before she bursts out laughing.

"Oh my god. You're never going to believe this."

"What?" I ask, wondering what could be worse than getting a tattoo and waking up wearing leather.

"Max..." she laughs, struggling to breathe. "He's been arrested... Again. He was found jaywalking naked from Hawthorn Farm."

She laughs, and I begin to laugh with her.

What the hell did we do last night?

Find out what they get up to in Max's novel, Book Four in the series.

ACKNOWLEDGMENTS

I never intended to write Evan's book. When I first began planning the Carter Brother series, Evan never even crossed my mind.

Then I released Mason, and I had so many people asking me if Evan was getting his own book. It got me thinking straight away. We already discovered there was something between Evan and his next-door neighbour, Lexi, but I wanted something more for him.

In came Kennedy.

She came to me in a dream, and I loved her character so much I decided to give her to Evan.

After that, the whole story pretty much came together by itself.

I didn't want to write a full novel for Evan due to the fact that this is a Carter Brother series, so I ended up going for a novella.

I honestly hope my readers enjoy his book and are looking forward to reading Max's. These characters have become such a huge part of my life that I feel like I live with them sometimes. Even my kids ask me what I have planned for them.

I want to thank everyone who has supported me, who helped me put this book together. Charlotte, for sticking by me and always listening to everything I have to say.

I want to thank my beta team for always reading and giving me back some fantastic pointers. You guys have been with me pretty much from the start, and are as much a part of this journey as anyone. You ladies rock!

To my fellow readers...

I don't even know where to begin. One minute, I was writing for fun, getting all these stories down for my own benefit, then the next,

I'm self-published and have so many followers I don't even know what to do with myself.

Many authors will agree and say they never expected to get this far, but hand on heart, I honestly didn't think I'd sell ten books, let alone what I do. It's been so overwhelming at times, and none of it feels real.

I try my best to reply to everyone who writes to me, and to acknowledge everyone who writes a review; good or bad.

So thank you. You've made my dream come true, and you continue to let it come true with every book of mine that you pick up and read. It means everything to me.

Thank you so much Stephanie Farrant for editing the new re-writes for these books. I'm forever grateful for you.

And a huge thank you to Harper at Dark City Designs. We can all agree she did an incredible job with the special editions. I am so honoured to have worked with her. These covers are beautiful and everything I ever wanted for them.

You can now find me at www.Lisahelengray.co.uk You'll also find a reading order on there too.

If you haven't already, please join my readers group: Lisa's Luscious Readers on Facebook.

ALSO BY LISA HELEN GRAY

Carter Brother Series

Malik ~ Book One

Mason ~ Book Two

Myles ~ Book Three

Evan ~ Book 3.5

Max ~ Book Four

Maverick ~ Book Five

Forgiven Series

Better Left Forgotten ~ Book One

Obsession ~ Book Two

Forgiven ~ Book Three

Whithall Series

Foul Play ~ Book One (Willow and Cole's Book)

Wish It Series

If I could I'd Wish It All Away ~ Book One (Standalone)

ABOUT THE AUTHOR

Lisa Helen Gray is Amazon's bestselling author of the Forgotten Series and Carter Brother series.

She loves hanging out, but most of all, curling up with a good book or watching movies. When she's not being a mom, she's been a writer and a blogger.

She loves writing romance novels, ones with a HEA and has a thing for alpha males.

I mean, who doesn't!

Just an ordinary girl surrounded by extraordinary books.

Printed in Great Britain
by Amazon

38044142R00097